Doggie humour is different from human humour. And I ... know, because I'm a dog! I sit under the table listening ... ew Cope chuckling as he writes his Spy Dog stories. ... he mostly writes about me, Lara. Or 'GM451' as he ...times calls me.

... book contains lots of jokes about me! Andrew read a ... to me, slapping his leg as he did so. I thought he was ... laugh his head off! And I listened politely but, like I sa..., canine jokes are a bit different.

... see, what I find funny is that Andrew Cope sometimes ... all night writing about me, while I snore as loudly as ... And then he works hard every day with school visits and ...ff while I laze around being the queen of cool. So, basi...y, he works every minute of every day while I lounge arou... having my tummy tickled. I get the praise. I get the fan ...l. He gets ignored! Now *that's* funny!

www.spydog451.co.uk

Books by Andrew Cope

Spy Dog
Spy Dog Captured!
Spy Dog Unleashed!
Spy Dog Superbrain
Spy Dog Rocket Rider
Spy Dog Secret Santa
Spy Dog Teacher's Pet
Spy Dog Joke Book

Spy Pups Treasure Quest
Spy Pups Prison Break
Spy Pups Circus Act
Spy Pups Danger Island

www.spydog451.co.uk

Andrew Cope

Illustrated by James de la Rue and Chris Mould

PUFFIN

PUFFIN BOOKS

Published by the Penguin Group
Penguin Books Ltd, 80 Strand, London WC2R 0RL, England
Penguin Group (USA) Inc., 375 Hudson Street, New York, New York 10014, USA
Penguin Group (Canada), 90 Eglinton Avenue East, Suite 700, Toronto, Ontario, Canada M4P 2Y3
(a division of Pearson Penguin Canada Inc.)
Penguin Ireland, 25 St Stephen's Green, Dublin 2, Ireland (a division of Penguin Books Ltd)
Penguin Group (Australia), 250 Camberwell Road, Camberwell, Victoria 3124, Australia
(a division of Pearson Australia Group Pty Ltd)
Penguin Books India Pvt Ltd, 11 Community Centre, Panchsheel Park, New Delhi – 110 017, India
Penguin Group (NZ), 67 Apollo Drive, Rosedale, Auckland 0632, New Zealand
(a division of Pearson New Zealand Ltd)
Penguin Books (South Africa) (Pty) Ltd, 24 Sturdee Avenue, Rosebank, Johannesburg 2196,
South Africa

Penguin Books Ltd, Registered Offices: 80 Strand, London WC2R 0RL, England

puffinbooks.com

First published 2011
001 – 10 9 8 7 6 5 4 3 2 1

Compiled and designed by Perfect Bound Ltd
Printed in Great Britain by Clays Ltd, St Ives plc

British Library Cataloguing in Publication Data
A CIP catalogue record for this book is available from the British Library

ISBN: 978–0–141–33621–3

www.greenpenguin.co.uk

To Grace and Sky
for putting up with a distracted dad

Contents

Initial Briefing

Welcome to the Secret Service, new agent. What you hold in your hands is extremely-very-super-top secret and must **NEVER** be revealed – keep it safe at all times! Don't worry too much about young members of the public seeing it, though – for some reason they seem to know all about LARA already. It's weird actually, it's almost as if someone has written whole books about her. As if that could happen!

No, it's Professor Cortex you've got to hide this book from. If he ever finds out we've been doodling on the GM451 files, and telling jokes about her amazing exploits, then we are in SERIOUS trouble.

He thinks we're all dead busy on lookout missions, tracking baddies and watching for trouble. But to be honest, a lot of this job is rather boring. You sit around in a van with some binoculars, some sandwiches and a big plastic bottle (don't ask what that's for) for hours and hours.

We have to do something to pass the time, or we'd end up as loopy as the prof. So we make up puzzles and gags to keep each other amused.

And then, to keep them secret from Professor Cortex, we hide our stuff in the *Spy Dog Mission Files* – which you need to see anyway, to give you all the info on GM451, our top Spy Dog. For instance, you do know what LARA stands for, don't you? What about her pups, STAR and SPUD? Oh dear. You'd better get reading then.

Just remember not to laugh too loud when the professor's about.

Agent D

CLASSIFIED

MISSION FILE

Ref: GM451/01/SPDG

BACKGROUND

GM451 is the first and most successful graduate from Professor Cortex's animal training programme. She is a Licensed Assault and Rescue Animal, or LARA for short. She successfully infiltrated a drug-smuggling operation, discovered vital evidence and managed to capture almost the entire gang by sinking their yacht. Sadly the gang leader, known to us as Mr Big, escaped. He immediately set out to destroy the dog that destroyed his criminal empire.

MISSION

GM451 followed her training and went into hiding. She got herself adopted from an RSPCA rescue centre by a normal family, the Cooks, and tried hard to blend in until we could track her down and bring her back to headquarters. Meanwhile, Mr Big was also trying to find GM451.

SUMMARY

GM451 failed in her attempts to act like a normal dog. The children of her cover family (Ben, Sophie and Ollie) soon realized she had special powers. She also failed to turn a blind eye to crime, and discovered another drugs gang. Cleverly she arranged for them to be captured without being identified herself. However Mr Big tracked GM451 down, determined to kill her.

CONCLUSIONS

The Cook children were involved in a dangerous situation, which must be avoided at all costs in the future. It is unlikely GM451 will ever recover fully from the wounds Mr Big inflicted.

PERSONAL FILE

Ref: GM451/HR001

Classification: Agent

Name: GM451, though her cover family call her Lara

Appearance: Labrador-sized mongrel: slim, white with some black patches. One ear sticks up, the other falls over her eye. Long whiskers and a floppy tongue.

Personality: Active, intelligent, inquisitive. Often ends up in dangerous situations because she doesn't think about the risks involved. Very caring and protective towards her cover family.

History: She was discovered as a youngster doing domestic chores for her owner, an old and ill man who needed professional care. Her family history is unknown.

Abilities: Almost limitless – if it can be done with paws, Lara can do it. Dancing, football, whistling, swimming, cycling, surfing, juggling, karate, computers, cooking . . .

Lara fell asleep with one eye open. She didn't sleep a wink.

Lara spent too long doing karate outdoors last winter. She caught kung flu.

How many hairs are there in Lara's tail?
None – they're all on the outside.

Where was Lara when the light went out?
In the dark.

Why does Lara turn round twice before she goes to sleep?
Because one good turn deserves another.

Lara fell off a ten-metre-tall ladder, but she wasn't hurt. She fell off the bottom rung.

What do you call Lara when she's stuck in the middle of a muddy track?
A mutt in a rut.

Why does Lara lie down?
Because she can't lie up.

You don't have to spend long in the Secret Service HQ before you start finding these cards lying about. Professor Cortex uses them to note his ideas for gadgets. Then he chucks out the ~~useless~~ 'less practical' ideas.

CORTEX BRAINDUMP 0001

PROBLEM:
Transporting small explosives into secure enemy areas.

SOLUTION:
Pigeons! Train them to carry and drop explosive eggs.

NEW PROBLEM:
It turns out pigeons are too stupid to train. They drop the eggs whenever they get bored, or scared.

NEW SOLUTION:
All personnel to be fitted with bomb-proof wigs?

Mission Log Extract

The next day, Lara was sitting on the toilet, legs crossed, reading the newspaper (like she'd seen Dad do), when Ollie burst into the bathroom. Lara thought it a bit rude that he should come in without knocking, but she carried on in the normal way, reaching for the toilet roll and wiping her doggie bottom.

Ollie looked dumbstruck. Having only just recently been toilet-trained himself, he was amazed to learn that Lara could wipe her own bottom. He still had to call Mum or Dad to help him.

Lara hadn't realized she had done anything out of the ordinary until Ollie piped up at teatime, 'Lara sat on the toilet to do her poo and I helped flush it because it was a big one.' The talk of poo and toilets caused Dad to put his knife and fork down, temporarily losing his appetite.

'Of course, Ollie,' said Mum, not taking a blind bit of notice, thinking that he was in one of his fantasy worlds again. 'She'll be sitting at the table, eating her dinner, next!'

The following day, Sophie caught Lara doing exactly that.

Spy Dog

What did the big toilet say to the little toilet?
You look a little flushed.

Who is the smelliest superhero?
Pooperman.

Why was Tigger staring into the toilet?
He was looking for Pooh.

Knock knock!
Who's there?
I done up.
I done up who?
Eww, really?
I didn't need to
know that!

People point to their wrists when they want to know the time. Why don't they point to their bums when they want to know where the toilet is?

Gran went to the doctor complaining that she was trumping a lot – dozens of times a day. 'It's annoying, but at least they're silent and don't smell,' she said. The doctor gave her some medicine and told her to come back in a week.

A week later Gran came back, terribly embarrassed. 'The medicine didn't work, Doctor. I'm still trumping, they're still silent, but now they smell terrible!'

'Great,' said the doctor. 'Now I've cleared your blocked nose, I can get your hearing tested.'

What do you call a smelly fairy?
Stinkerbell.

How does Lara take a toilet break when she's on the computer?
She uses weemail.

How do trees get on to the Internet?
Easy, they just log on.

Oh no, my computer's frozen again!
Maybe you should take it out of the fridge.

Why did the computer sneeze?
It had caught a virus.

Mission Log Extract

Lara entered a new password she had recently set up and opened her email account. Typing is difficult for a dog, what with having clumsy paws instead of hands, so she found it quicker and easier to tap out the words using a pencil held in her mouth. She rushed the typing, so it wasn't perfect; but when she thought about it, it wasn't bad for a dog.

deer policE. There R some dRug dealers locked in a giant FRidge at Harrys Quality Meat WarEHouse on Station ROAd. There R 46 sacks of Drugs on the premiSes and a dog called Bruce gArding the eEExit. Pleas3 hurry or Bruces owner will LOSe patience and he will b in tGrouble. Please bring blankets 4 tHe men will b very cold

Tha4NKs.

Spy Dog

Why did the computer squeak?
Somebody squeezed its mouse.

What did the computer do for lunch?
It went for a byte.

'Mum, Dad's broken the computer!'
'How did he do that?'
'I threw it at his head.'

What did the girl keyboard say to the boy keyboard?
'Sorry, you're not my type.'

Dad entered a competition to win a year's supply of Marmite. He won, and got sent one jar.

Mum got an exercise DVD but thought it sounded too difficult – the back said 'Running Time 90 minutes' and she didn't think she could run that long.

For Valentine's Day, Dad cooked Mum a candlelit dinner. She hated it – the food was barely warm and all smoky.

Dad went to a second-hand shop, but they couldn't help him. He wanted one for his watch.

Dad came home very angry with Mum. 'I've found out you've been telling people I'm an idiot!'

'I'm sorry,' replied Mum. 'I didn't know it was meant to be a secret.'

'Did you hear what Dad said when he stepped in that dog poo?'

'Yes . . . shall I leave out the swearing?'

'Yes, please.'

'Then he didn't say anything.'

Dad came home covered in bruises. He had started to go through a revolving door and changed his mind.

Mission Log Extract

Ben explained to Sophie and Ollie how they could communicate with Lara by asking a series of 'yes' and 'no' questions. 'She can't speak, but she can understand. She will shake or nod if you ask "yes" or "no" questions. Try it.'

Sophie composed herself and tried to think of a question to ask. 'Lara, are you special?' she began.

Nod.

Sophie glanced up at her brother, to see him grinning just as much as she was.

'Can you understand me?'

Vigorous nod.

'Can you understand Ben?'

Very big nod. Lara looked at Ben and winked.

'Can you understand Ollie?'

Shrug that meant: *Sometimes, but he does talk some rubbish.*

'Why are you special? Oh no, you can't answer that because you can't talk. Erm, are you allowed to let grown-ups know you're special?'

Big shake of the head. *Certainly not, or they'd get me on the telly, and then the baddies might come after me.*

Spy Dog

'Dad, why are we still waiting for dinner?'

'I'm sorry, love, but the salt cellar was empty.'

'Why does that mean dinner is late?'

'It's taken me ages to refill it through that little hole.'

PERSONAL FILE

Ref: GM451/BDY0001

Classification: Serious Villain

Name: Mr Big

Appearance: Tall, well-built male. Short dark hair, narrow sideburns and a goatee beard. Dark brown eyes.

Personality: Intelligent and quick-thinking, but impulsive and has a short temper. Thinks he's better than most people, which makes him sarcastic and cruel. Can be violent.

History: Ran a global drugs empire until it was destroyed by GM451. Has worked non-stop to destroy her in revenge ever since.

Identification: First exposed by GM451, who gave him significant injuries to his ~~upper rear thigh~~ bum.

Crime: Apart from the drugs, Mr Big is guilty of criminal damage, kidnap, deception, firearms offences, dangerous driving with intent to cause injury and the attempted murder of a Licensed Assault and Rescue Animal.

Mr Big came back to his car to find it badly dented with a broken headlight. Tucked under the wiper was a note that read, 'Sorry, I just reversed into your car. There are people watching me who think I'm leaving you my name and address. But I'm not.'

Mr Big tried shoplifting once, but he had to stop.
He strained his back trying to pick up a garage.

Mr Big robbed an ice-cream van.
He got away with hundreds and thousands.

Mr Big got hold of some fake money, but it wasn't very good, so he was worried about using it. He went to a little shop in a quiet village. 'Can you change this eighteen-pound note for me?' he asked.

The old shopkeeper smiled. 'Certainly. I can give you three six-pound notes or two nines.'

Mr Big held up a shop once.
It was easy - it was a paper shop.

Mr Big got caught stealing full stops.
He's going to get a very long sentence.

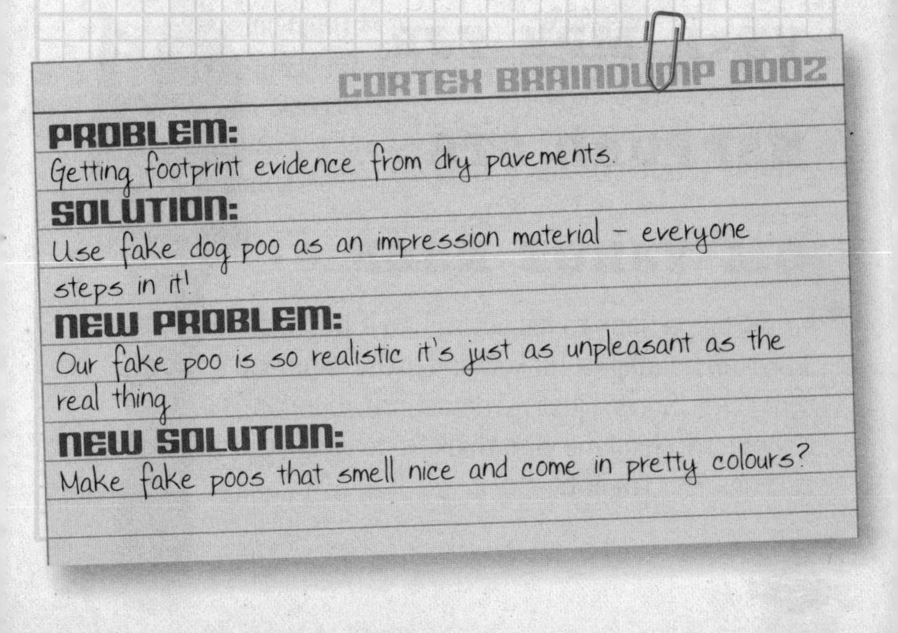

Keyboard Konundrum

Agents need to be able to type quickly and accurately. Familiarize yourself with this standard keyboard.

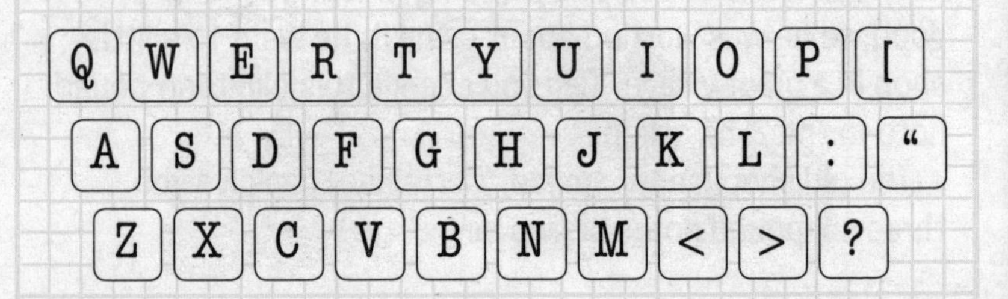

Below is a secret message that has been typed wrongly – instead of the correct letter, the key just to the right was hit instead. (For example, E was typed instead of W.) What should the message read?

VP<R MPE YJR

NSFFORD STR

OM YJROT NSDR

Brain XLR8R Test 01

Agents need to think clearly and quickly. These puzzles are meant to make your brain work better – if you think in dull, obvious ways you'll get them wrong!

1) What is full of holes but still holds water?

2) How could all of your cousins have an aunt who is not your aunt?

3) You have 10p and a one-pound coin, to buy a tag and a collar. The tag costs one pound more than the collar. How much is the collar?

4) What can run but never walks, has a mouth but never talks, has a head but never weeps, and has a bed but never sleeps?

5) Can you use the letters in NEW DOOR to make one word?

6) What is as light as a feather, but not even the strongest man can hold it for more than a few minutes?

7) There's something in a car engine that serves no purpose, but without it the engine doesn't work. What is it?

8) Johnny's mum has four children. Her first was called April, the second was called May and the third was called June. What is her fourth child's name?

ANSWERS ON PAGE 134

CLASSIFIED

MISSION FILE

Ref: GM451/02/CPTRD

BACKGROUND

GM451 recovered from her injuries, but never became fit enough to return to full active duty. She remained undercover with the Cook family, under strict instructions not to draw attention to herself. *Not that she listened!*

MISSION

We discovered GM451 was being watched. To keep her safe, she and the Cooks were sent to an isolated location – the seaside. While there she was asked to investigate a series of dognappings.

Not that bright

SUMMARY

The criminals were quickly identified, but GM451 struggled to keep the Cook children and their cousins safe while watching the thieves. A photographer who had been spying on GM451 made the mission more complicated by joining the dog-stealing gang.

CONCLUSIONS

GM451 persuaded one gang member to drug the other two, and alerted Professor Cortex to come to the rescue. Some of the children were accidentally taken by the dognappers, but GM451 managed to rescue them safely.

Mission Log Extract

Eventually the children reached the far end of the beach, deserted of holidaymakers who didn't want to walk too far for an ice cream. But it was perfect for Lara to try her paw at surfing. The conditions were ideal, a rough sea throwing up good surf and the perfect setting, with golden sand backed by steep cliffs. Ben, Sophie, Adam and Hayley squeezed into their wetsuits and then the children and Lara raced into the waves with their boards. They were all expert swimmers and spent the next two hours clowning about in the water, toppling off waves and generally exhausting themselves. Surfing was a lot harder than it looked. Hayley just about managed to mount her surfboard once, while her brother and cousins failed dismally. Lara was the only one to get the hang of it and she gleefully rode several waves, howling with delight and punching the air every time. *What a holiday! What a triumph! What an achievement for the canine species!*

Spy Dog Captured!

What do trees wear at the seaside?
Swimming trunks.

What did the sea say to the beach?
Nothing, it just gave a little wave.

Why had Sophie had enough of surfing after an hour?
Because she'd got a little board.

Why do dolphins swim in salt water?
Because pepper makes them sneeze.

What hairstyle does the sea have?
Wavy.

Why did the whale cross the sea?
To get to the other tide.

Why is it easy to weigh fish?
They come with their own scales.

I've got two octopuses that look exactly alike.
I think they may be i-tentacle.

What do you get on a very little beach?
Micro-waves.

What do you get if you cross a snowman and a shark?
Frostbite.

Why didn't the mussel have any friends?
Because he was a little shellfish.

Ben has had a number of girlfriends since he started secondary school. And that number is 'zero'.

Who's that girl at school that won't give Ben her name? **Chantelle.**

For some reason Ollie gave Ben a big lump of plasticine for his birthday.
He doesn't know what to make of it.

PERSONAL FILE

Ref: GM451/FMLY003

Classification: Approved Associate

Name: Ben Cook

Appearance: Slim, fair hair, large ears. Good-looking lad, tall for his age.

Personality: Highly intelligent, good sense of humour, terrible dancer. Shy but brave and loyal to his friends.

History: Ben and his family adopted GM451 from the RSPCA shelter while she was hiding from Mr Big (see Mission GM451/001/SPDG page 3). He continues to be her primary carer following her injuries – and her main human partner in a continuing series of risky missions.

Ben got told off for messing about in a lesson and had to stand outside. He got really embarrassed - it was a swimming lesson.

Ben asked Dad for some help with his homework.

'I don't know, son,' replied Dad. 'It wouldn't really be right, would it?'

'I know it won't,' said Ben. 'But have a go anyway.'

Dad asked Ben to stand behind the car and tell him if the indicators were working.

'OK, Dad,' replied Ben. 'Yes . . . no; yes . . . no; yes . . . no; yes . . . no . . .'

Ben always knows when Mum feels cold because she tells him to put on a jumper.

CORTEX BRAINDUMP 0003

PROBLEM:
How to control very aggressive dogs.

SOLUTION:
Electric-shock dog collar.

NEW PROBLEM:
Getting near enough to the dangerous dog to put the collar on.

NEW SOLUTION:
Big iron gloves? Not sure. Maybe GM451 can manage this.

Mission Log Extract

The trio roared through the night, the motorbike eating up the road. Ben spotted the lorry in the distance. 'There it is, up ahead,' he shouted above the noise of the Harley.

I see it, acknowledged Lara, *but I'm not quite sure what we're going to do when we catch up*.

The lumbering lorry soon came into range and the biker-three cruised behind. Ben, sitting at the front, was proving to be an expert with steering and acceleration. Lara, at the back, was superb at gear changes. Adam, the sandwich filling, still couldn't quite believe what was happening. He was gripping Ben so tightly that it was affecting his circulation.

Three miles to the motorway, Lara noticed from a sign. *I think this is time for action*. She tightened her helmet strap and pulled the goggles over her eyes. *This could get a bit hairy*.

Spy Dog Captured!

When is a car not a car?
When it turns into a side road.

Dad went to look for a new car, but he didn't have a lot of money. He found one he liked, but was confused when the salesman brought out a pair of hiking boots when Dad said he'd buy it.

'These come free with the car,' said the salesman.

'But what are they for?' asked Dad.

'Well, you're going to be walking home a lot.'

What should you do if you see a spaceman when you're driving?
Park in it, man.

Bill was caught speeding, and went to court for sentencing. 'I'll leave the choice of punishment up to you,' said the judge. 'Thirty days in prison or £300.'

Bill thought for a moment. 'I'd like the money, please.'

What's the most dangerous part of a motorbike?
The nut that connects the seat to the handlebars.

Dad called Gran on her mobile.

'You need to be careful. I've just heard on the news that someone was driving the wrong way round the ring road earlier!'

'It wasn't just one car, dear,' said Gran. 'It was all of them!'

Driving on holiday Mum had to get the tyres pumped up. 'How much is that?' she asked the attendant.

'Ten pounds,' came the reply.

'Ten pounds! That's a lot for some air!' said Mum.

'Well, that's inflation for you.'

PERSONAL FILE

Ref: GM451/BDY0002/3

Classification: Villains

Names: Bill and Ned

Appearance: Bill – fat, short and balding, tattoos on neck and knuckles. Ned – tall and thin with a bad stutter.

Personality: Bill – lazy, greedy bully. Ned – weak-willed, not essentially criminal but easily persuaded; a dog lover. Neither trusts the other.

History: Valuable dogs were being kidnapped at various locations and sold for profit. When dogs started going missing where GM451 was going on holiday, she was asked to help.

Identification: GM451 came across the pair who were drunk in a pub, revealing they were kidnapping dogs.

Bill is really lazy. If he drops something, he won't pick it up until his laces need tying.

Bill works almost every day. He almost works on Monday, then almost works on Tuesday, then almost works on Wednesday . . .

Ned went to a speech therapist who spent a week trying to cure his stutter. Bill asked him how it was going.

'Peter Piper picked a peck of pickled peppers,' said Ned.

'Wow, that's pretty good,' said Bill.

'Y-y-yes, b-b-b-but it's p-p-p-p-pretty hard t-t-t-to g-g-get that into a c-c-c-c-conversation.'

CORTEX BRAINDUMP 004

PROBLEM:
Dogs can't talk.

SOLUTION:
Dog biscuits with letters on – Lara can spell out words with them.

NEW PROBLEM:
Lara eats the biscuits and can't spell anything useful with the ones that are left.

NEW SOLUTION:
Hmm. Dog biscuits that taste horrible so dogs won't eat them?

Mission Log Extract

Bill's stomach was swollen with wind and the pain was terrible. It came in waves and when his guts signalled go, it really was time to go. He clenched his bottom, but he couldn't hold the pressure as another eruption of wind nearly raised him off the driving seat. He wound down the window, wafting his hand across his face to hasten the clearing of the smell.

Spy Dog Captured!

What musical instrument can Bill play?
The trump-et.

What are invisible and smell of bananas?
Monkey farts.

Why do farts smell?
So deaf people get to enjoy them too.

Did you hear about the short-sighted skunk?
He fell in love with a fart.

DOG TANGLE

These dog names have been mixed up. Can you work out what they should be?

REWRITELOT

HANDSCUD

LARBOARD

RIVERTREE

BAGEEL

ORBEX

BOGDULL

MANILATAD

UCUHIHAHA

YONDERHUG

Brain XLR8R Test 02

Time for your next round of brain stretching. Read the questions carefully.

1) If the Professor had 19 pigs and all but five ran away, how many would he have left?

2) Take 3 oranges from 4 oranges and what do you have?

3) Divide 40 by half and add 10. What do you get?

4) A vet gives you 3 pills for your cat and tells you to give the cat a pill every half-hour. How long will they last?

5) January has 31 days, September has 30 days. How many months of the year have 28 days?

6) How many animals of each species did Moses take on the ark?

7) Which is correct:
The yolk of an egg **is** white?
The yolk of an egg **are** white?

8) You are driving a bus picking passengers up at Glasgow Bus Station. Six passengers get on. The bus drives to Edinburgh where four get off and two get on. The bus then goes to Dundee where four get off and five get on. The bus returns to Glasgow where three get off and two get on. What's the name of the driver?

ANSWERS ON PAGE 134

CLASSIFIED

MISSION FILE

Ref: GM451/03/NLSHD

BACKGROUND

Mr Big was safely in prison. He continued to plot his revenge on GM451, who was taking a holiday with her cover family. She continued to draw attention to herself. At home she began training local pets to form an animal neighbourhood watch.

Doing a pretty good job, too

MISSION

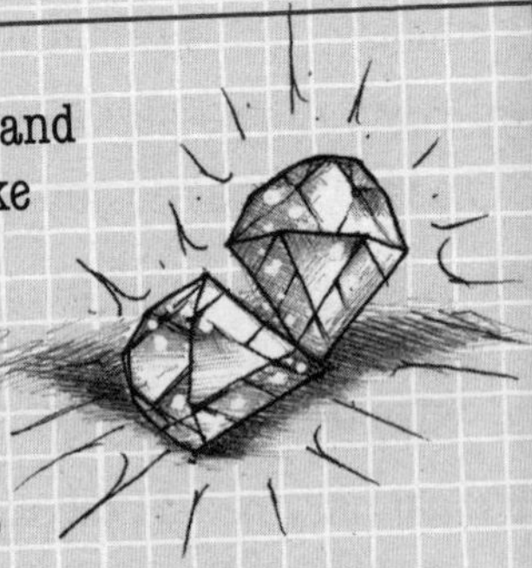

Three prisoners escaped from prison, and a few weeks later a dog looking just like GM451 started a mini crime-wave. The police arrested and jailed her. Meanwhile a mysterious millionaire announced he was going to exhibit the Millennium Diamond at the Natural History Museum.

SUMMARY

Professor Cortex and the Cook children helped GM451 escape, and she directed them to the museum. They managed to foil the theft of the Millennium Diamond – and trap the thieves.

(We helped a bit)

CONCLUSIONS

Yet again GM451 put the Cook children at risk, which upset their mother a great deal. Firearms were discharged, and a vehicle crashed. The children were lucky to avoid injury, but were crucial to the mission's success.

Mrs Cook is good at shouting

Mission Log Extract

Mr Peacock couldn't help but look. He could see the top of a chef's hat. As he walked on and the hedge dipped he could gradually see more of the hat – and the wearer. He spied an ear, a furry one with a hole in. His eye was twitching alarmingly now as he stopped in his tracks and shook his head. This walk was meant to clear his head of waterskiing, cricketing dogs and now here was a pooch chef. He gawped over the hedge and saw Lara cooking sausages and burgers on the barbie. He twitched in amazement as the mutt sauntered over to a deckchair and picked up a book. She fixed her glasses on the end of her nose and settled into a good read, noisily sipping the last of her milkshake.

Ahh, perfect, she thought. *Shaken not stirred. Just the way I like it.*

Mr Peacock quickened his pace in an effort to catch up with his wife. 'Margaret,' he shouted, 'I think I need to see a doctor.'

Spy Dog Unleashed!

'Doctor, I've got a strawberry growing out of my forehead.'
'Oh, I've got some cream for that.'

'I'm pleased your cough sounds better this morning.'
'It should do, Doctor – I've been practising all night.'

'Doctor, I've got mashed potato in my ears and a sausage stuck up my nose.'
'I don't think you've been eating right.'

'Doctor, I think I need glasses.'
'You certainly do, this is a fish and chip shop.'

'Doctor, I'm so stressed that I keep losing my temper.'
'OK, tell me all about it.'
'I just did, you stupid little man!'

'Doctor, I'm worried my hair is falling out. Can you give me something to keep it in?'
'Sure – here's a shoebox.'

Mr Peacock went to the doctor's, complaining that he hurt all over his body.

'Really?' said the doctor. 'Show me what you mean.'

Mr Peacock touched his knee and yelled, 'Ouch, that hurts!' He touched his stomach and groaned, 'Oww ow ow!!' Then he touched his ear. 'Ouch, even that hurts!'

'I think I know what the problem is, Mr Peacock,' said the doctor. 'You've broken your finger.'

PERSONAL FILE

Ref: GM451/BDY0004/5

Classification: Villains

Names: Gus and Archie

Appearance: Gus – huge and strong, shaved head, lots of tattoos, gold teeth. Archie – skinny and very hairy, with a red face and small features.

Personality: Career criminals – lazy and greedy. Gus uses his muscles, Archie his brains.

History: The pair met Mr Big while in prison and were easily persuaded to join him in his latest plan – to punish GM451 and get extremely rich.

Identification: Gus and Archie were spotted in the act of stealing the Millennium Diamond.

Crimes: Attempted theft, deception, dangerous driving, criminal damage . . .

Archie was very annoyed to be given a speeding ticket. 'What am I meant to do with this?' he shouted.

'Keep it,' replied the policeman. 'When you collect four of them, you get a bicycle.'

Gus used to have a Dutch girlfriend who wore inflatable shoes. One day he heard the sad news that she'd popped her clogs.

CORTEX BRAINDUMP 0005

PROBLEM:

GM451 needs non-violent ways to immobilize villains.

SOLUTION:

Pills that produce instant sleep.

NEW PROBLEM:

Could be very dangerous – while driving, for instance.

NEW SOLUTION:

Pills that give you the runs? Or would that be even worse when driving?

Archie went to the barber's. 'I'd like my hair long on one side, please,' he asked. 'Cut the other side ragged and short, leave bits sticking out on top and scrape the back of my neck with a blunt razor.'

'Wow, that sounds quite tricky,' said the barber. 'I'm not sure I can do that.'

'Well you did it last time I came,' replied Archie.

Gus parks his car next to a traffic warden. 'If I park on these double yellow lines and nip over the road for a minute, will you give me a parking ticket?' he asks.

'Of course I will,' replies the warden.

'That's not fair,' complains Gus. 'There's other cars parked here and you haven't ticketed them yet.'

'I know, but none of them asked me for a ticket.'

'Nice suit, Archie,' said Gus. 'It's Italian, isn't it?'

'Yes, it is,' gasped Archie. 'How on earth can you tell?'

'Because it's got spaghetti Bolognese all down the front,' replied Gus.

Mission Log Extract

Lara was home alone, but, as always, she tried to use her time wisely. Her latest mission was to organize the local pets into a neighbourhood-watch team. The assorted group of dogs and cats assembled on Tuesday and Thursday mornings to be put through their paces. George the tortoise always came too, usually setting off hours before, to get to the meetings on time. Lara wasn't quite sure how he'd ever come in useful, but she couldn't fault his positive attitude. The dogs and cats still eyed each other suspiciously. Lara had told them to put their differences aside for the sake of teamwork but Rex the Alsatian couldn't help licking his lips every time he looked at next door's tabby.

Spy Dog Unleashed!

What do the neighbourhood watch call the woman who's always hanging out washing?
Peggy.

What do they call the man with the big pile of leaves in his garden?
Russell.

What do they call the man carrying a plank of wood on his head?
Edward.

Why should you be careful when it's raining cats and dogs?
Because you might step in a poodle.

When they advertise a new improved dog food that tastes better, how do they know? Who tries it?

How can a tortoise make a sound like a cat?
Put it on a rocket-powered skateboard. Meeeeeeeyoooooowwwww!

What's the difference between cats and dogs?
Dogs have owners, cats have staff.

A man went into a cafe with a tortoise on his head. The waitress gave him a coffee and said, 'Why have you got a tortoise on your head?'

'I always wear a tortoise on my head on Tuesdays,' replied the man.

'Today's Wednesday,' said the waitress.

'Oh no! Really? Wow, I must look such an idiot.'

PERSONAL FILE

Ref: GM451/FMLY004

Classification: Approved Associate

Name: Sophie Cook

Appearance: Mousy hair, freckles across her nose, shortish for her age. Two years younger than Ben.

Personality: Sparky, giggly and clever. Very protective of her brothers.

History: Sophie loves GM451, and appreciates the help she gets with her homework. She is slightly more sensible than her brother Ben, but has managed to get into almost as much trouble.

One of Sophie's friends is so skinny, she wears a one-one to her ballet class.

Another of her friends has two left feet. When she goes on holiday, she wears flip-flips.

Sophie and Lara were playing cards on holiday in their tent when a man walked past and stopped, open-mouthed.

'Wow, that's amazing! What a smart dog,' he exclaimed.

'Not really,' said Sophie. 'When she gets a good hand, she wags her tail.'

Sophie got into an argument with a nasty neighbour.

'And you can keep that horrible mutt of yours out of my house!' yelled the woman. 'It's crawling with fleas!'

'Do you hear, Lara?' said Sophie. 'Stay out of her house – it's full of fleas.'

'Sophie, did your father help with this homework?'
'No, sir. I got it wrong all by myself.'

'Warm milk makes me sleepy,' complained Sophie, 'but cold milk wakes me up.'

'How come?' asked Ben.

'The milkman delivers at four in the morning.'

Sophie sees Ollie with a bag of doughnuts. 'Ollie, if I can guess how many doughnuts you've got, will you give me one?'

'If you can guess right, I'll give you both of them.'

CORTEX BRAINDUMP 0006

PROBLEM:
How can we pass messages to GM451 without anyone noticing?

SOLUTION:
Robot fleas that can record and play back messages direct into her ear.

NEW PROBLEM:
The fleas make GM451 itch. She scratches them off and we lose them. And they cost £1 million each.

NEW SOLUTION:
A hollow fake bone that unscrews into two halves. Simple – and cheap!

Mission Log Extract

Lara and the professor stood in the entrance hall and marvelled at the scene. The dog let out a low whistle of amazement. *Wow. What a place!* The huge hall was dominated by the dinosaur skeleton that towered above them. There was an eerie silence, except for their footsteps echoing. Lara spotted an arrow pointing to the Millennium Diamond Exhibition and the professor followed her along a long, dark corridor. She turned into a room marked 'Creatures of the Sea' and they wandered in awe past an unimaginably huge blue whale. The professor opened one of the windows and beckoned to the children outside. They came running and quickly clambered in while the policeman wasn't looking.

Spy Dog Unleashed!

Why do museums have old dinosaur bones?
They can't afford new ones.

Where does the museum go to weigh its whale?
The whale-weigh station.

Why did the dinosaur cross the road?
Because the chicken hadn't evolved yet.

Dad went into the Natural History Museum and stopped one of the guards. 'Do you have dinosaur bones?' he asked.

'No,' said the guard. 'I'm just a bit stiff after going to the gym.'

What do you call a dinosaur with no eyes?
Dyouthinkhesaurus.

What do triceratops sit on?
Tricerabottoms.

What makes more noise than a hungry dinosaur?
Two hungry dinosaurs.

Which dinosaur could jump higher than a house?
All of them – houses can't jump.

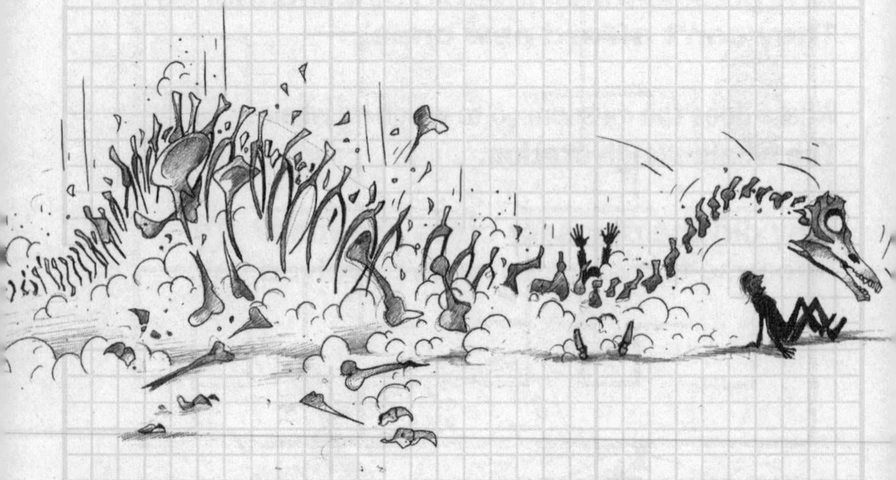

MUSEUM MAZE

Guide Lara through the museum to the room with the Millennium Diamond, and on to the exit without getting caught.

ANSWER ON PAGE 134

ODD Lara OUt

The villains used an evil dog that looked exactly like Lara to get her into trouble. Can you work out which of these dogs is not Lara, but the lookalike?

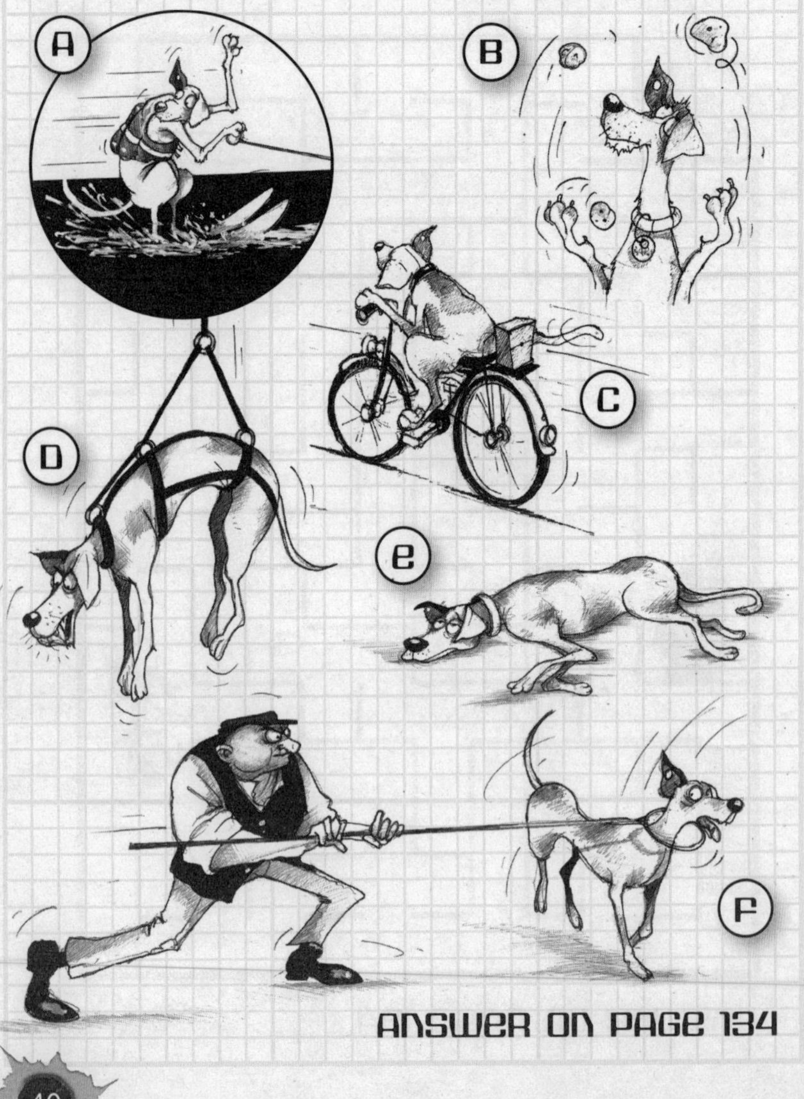

ANSWER ON PAGE 134

CLASSIFIED

MISSION FILE

Ref: GM451/04/SPRBRN

BACKGROUND

A group of secondary-school teachers, led by Dame Payne, were searching their school for a bright child – more specifically, a bright child's brain. They needed it for a formula that would make people super-intelligent, which they were going to sell.

Very cruel & bossy

MISSION

They changed their plans when they discovered Professor Cortex had already invented his own version, and sent a young man, Christopher Bent, to steal the professor's brain formula. Bent double-crossed the teachers and took the formula himself. When the teachers found out, they kidnapped the professor and forced him to make his brain formula for them. GM451 tracked down the professor and set off in pursuit.

Bent: total thicko, v. greedy

SUMMARY

The criminals started to double-cross each other and the situation became confused and risky. Unfortunately, the Cook children were with GM451, and were in grave danger as the chase came to a violent end.

Should have guessed Payne had a gun!

CONCLUSIONS

Justified risks were taken, but innocent people were placed in danger, and agents were injured. This must not happen again.

PERSONAL FILE

Ref: GM451/BDY0006

Classification: Villain

Name: Christopher Bent

Appearance: Skinny teenager, short hair, multiple piercings in ears, nose, etc.

Personality: Greedy, uneducated, unskilled, unambitious, poor sense of hygiene.

History: Recruited by Dame Payne on the basis of prior association with fellow evil teacher Mr Wilde.

Crime: Stole secret brain formula; won TV quiz as a result. Assisted in abduction of Professor Cortex.

Christopher Bent soon lost all the money he won.
He bought thousands of trumpets and blew the lot.

Christopher got a job at the factory that makes M&M's, but he soon got fired.
He was throwing out all the Ws.

How do you change Christopher Bent's mind?
Blow in his ear.

How do you make Christopher Bent laugh on a Wednesday?
Tell him a joke on a Monday.

Christopher Bent is so stupid that . . .

. . . he spent an hour looking at a carton of orange juice, just because it said 'Concentrate'.

. . . when he got annoyed with his goldfish, he tried to drown it.

. . . when he missed the number 22 bus, he got on a number 11 twice instead.

. . . when he saw a sign saying 'CAUTION - WET FLOOR' he did a wee.

. . . when he heard most accidents happen at home, he moved house.

. . . when the phone rang while he was ironing, he burnt his ear.

. . . he complained about a doughnut he'd bought because it had a hole in it.

. . . when he tripped and fell down the stairs, he got lost halfway.

. . . he asked for a refund on a jigsaw puzzle, because it was broken.

. . . he cut holes in his umbrella so he could see if it was raining.

Why does Christopher Bent smile at lightning?
He thinks someone is taking his picture.

CORTEX BRAINDUMP 0007

PROBLEM:
Glasses keep disappearing

SOLUTION:
Homing device fitted to glasses, linked to a tracker thingy that bleeps to find the glasses

NEW PROBLEM:
Can't find the tracker thingy!

NEW SOLUTION:
Fit a homing device to the tracker thingy, linked to another tracker thingy. Then if I lose that tracker thingy I can . . . ah. More thought needed!

Mission Log Extract

Dame Payne stood tall and gathered her black robes, flapping like a raven. She looked out at the sea of faces and wondered which child would become the superbrain.

'Blimey, check out her outfit. Looks like she thinks this is Hogwarts,' sniggered Toby Ward from Year Eight.

Dame Payne's hearing was as sharp as her temper. She pointed a warning finger at Toby. 'You, boy!' she shouted. 'The one laughing.'

Toby blushed. 'Who, me, Miss?' he mouthed, looking around innocently.

'Yes, you, lad,' bellowed the new head. 'Out. Now. Pack your bags, clear your desk. You're finished.'

'But . . .' began Toby. 'I've not done nothing.'

'No. You haven't done *anything*,' corrected Dame Payne.

'Exactly,' agreed Toby Ward.

'Don't get clever with me, Sonny Jim,' warned the stern-faced head teacher. 'Did I ask you to answer back? No, I don't think I did. Goodbye, Mr Trouble.'

Spy Dog Superbrain

'Oh, my teacher's such an idiot.'
'Really? Do you know who I am? I'm your teacher's daughter.'
'Ah. Do you know who I am?'
'No, I don't.'
'Thank goodness for that!'

'If you had one pound and asked your dad for another pound, how much would you have?'
'One pound.'
'Oh dear, you don't know your arithmetic.'
'No, you don't know my father.'

'Right, class, in this box I have a ten-foot snake.'
'Oh no, you don't, sir, snakes don't have feet!'

'I hope I didn't see you looking at Ben's answers.'
'I hope you didn't either.'

Ben put his hand up in class. 'Sir, can you tell me why the word "phonics" isn't spelt the way it sounds?'

One kid at Ben's old school was really naughty. His parents were called into school so often they had a better attendance record than he did.

'Dad, I hope I live a really long, long life.'
'Why's that, Ben?'
'Because it's the only way I'm going to get through all this homework.'

PERSONAL FILE

Ref: GM451/FMLY005

Classification: Approved Associate

Name: Ollie

Appearance: Stocky with fair hair. Four years younger than Ben, two years younger than Sophie.

Personality: Ollie has an unusual view of life and finds odd humour in the strangest situations. He loves his food.

History: Ollie was still very young when GM451 joined the Cook family and wasn't able to join in fully with her earlier adventures. More recently he has been very enthusiastic to play a full part, which frightens his sister sometimes.

Dad was reading the paper when Ollie waved a hand in his face, shouting, 'Look at this, Daddy!'

Humouring his son, Dad grabbed Ollie's fingers, put them in his mouth and growled, 'Daddy's going to eat your fingers!'

Ollie ran off giggling, but came back five minutes later looking annoyed.

'What's the matter, Ollie?' asked Dad.

'Daddy, where's my bogey gone?'

'Ollie, how do you always end up so dirty?'
'Well, I'm nearer the ground than you.'

Ollie took ages trying to work out how his seat belt did up.
Then all of a sudden it clicked.

'Ollie, stop pulling that cat's tail!'
'I'm not pulling, I'm holding. The cat's doing the pulling.'

A salesman saw Ollie sitting on the doorstep. 'Is your mum in, lad?' he asked.
'Yes,' smiled Ollie. So the salesman stepped up and rang the doorbell. He waited and waited, but there was no answer.
'I thought you said your mum was in,' he grumbled.
'She is,' replied Ollie. 'But this isn't my house.'

'Ollie,' asked Ben. 'Do you ever exaggerate?'
'Never,' replied Ollie. 'Never, ever, ever.'

Ollie asked his mum how long it was until Christmas.
'Why do you want to know?' she replied.
'I need to know if I have to start being good yet.'

CORTEX BRAINDUMP 0008

PROBLEM:
Hiding a camera quickly in a public place.

SOLUTION:
Dog-poo-cam! Looks and feels (who tested that?) like the real thing; contains a small video camera.

NEW PROBLEM:
Council cleaners keep doing their job. We've got lots of footage of the inside of bins!

NEW SOLUTION:
Add a small speaker and a recording: 'Please leave this poo where you found it!'

What was the first thing the Queen did when she came to the throne?
She sat down.

The Queen was showing Barack Obama her stables when one of the horses trumped.

'Oh dear,' said the Queen. 'How embarrassing. I'm terribly sorry about that.'

'Don't worry about it, ma'am,' replied Obama. 'To be honest, I thought it was the horse.'

Mission Log Extract

'Your Majesty, I'd like you to meet our youngest, Oliver. He's only four but played an important role in capturing the villains.'

The Queen bent down and her face broke into a warm royal smile. She took Ollie's hand and shook it. Ollie thought he saw her smile fade as she felt something sticky on the end of his finger. She quickly got out a hankie from the small bag she was carrying. Then she opened her mouth to speak, but Ollie couldn't wait to be spoken to. 'You look just like the lady on the stamps,' he beamed. The Queen opened her mouth again, but Ollie carried on. 'And I've been wondering – have you got a PlayStation? I bet you've got every game in the world,' he added. 'And have you ever had anyone's head chopped off?'

'That's a lot of questions,' said the Queen.

Spy Dog Superbrain

When her children get into trouble, does the Queen have a bad heir day?

The Royal Wedding came just in time at Ben's house. They really needed some new tea towels and coffee mugs.

The Queen was hosting an important banquet. The food was delicious, so she was surprised to see that the two men next to her were sneakily eating sandwiches they had hidden in their pockets.

'I'm sorry,' she whispered to them, 'but would you mind not eating your own food?'

The two men looked at each other, shrugged . . . and swapped sandwiches.

Mission Log Extract

Dad approached the customer services lady and cleared his throat. 'Erm, hello,' the others heard him say. 'This may sound like a strange request, but –' Dad hesitated while he re-read the note – 'we're looking for an unusual pet.'

The customer services lady smiled at him. 'What kind of unusual?' she asked.

Dad consulted his note once more. He looked round at the family again, feeling a little stupid. *Go on*, thought Lara, *spit it out, man. This is the code that gets us in. You have to get it right.*

'Have you got any . . . zebras?' Dad blurted, ignoring Ollie's snort behind him. 'Er, yes, zebras,' repeated Dad, looking down at his note again. 'A male one,' he added. 'Black with white stripes.'

'Not a female?' asked the lady. 'Are you sure?'

Dad consulted the note one last time. 'No, they would be white with black stripes. We definitely don't want one of those,' he read stiffly.

Spy Dog Superbrain

What do you call a zebra at the North Pole?
Lost.

A deer was trying to cross a busy road, but the traffic was so heavy he couldn't get across. A bear walking by said to him, 'If it's any help, there's a zebra crossing just down the road.'

'Really?' replied the deer. 'I hope he's having better luck than I am.'

An explorer in the jungle saw a monkey carrying a tin opener. Laughing, he called out, 'You don't need a tin opener to open a banana!'

'Don't be stupid,' replied the monkey. 'This is for the custard.'

What's white and goes 'RRRRG! RRRRG!'?
A polar bear walking backwards.

What did the father buffalo say when he left his son?
'Bison.'

What do polar bears call explorers in sleeping bags?
Sandwiches.

Why do elephants have four feet?
They'd look silly with five centimetres.

Two giraffes had a race. It was very close – they were neck and neck.

Why did the hippopotamus fall out of the tree?
The elephant pushed him out.

Brain XLR8R Test 03

By now your brain should be beginning to expand and work harder. See if you can manage these advanced puzzles.

1) Why can't a woman living in Wales be buried in England?

2) Peacocks are birds that don't lay eggs. So where do baby peacocks come from?

3) Eskimos are very good hunters, but they never hunt penguins. Why not?

4) Which is heavier, a ton of lead or a ton of feathers?

5) How far can you walk into the woods?

6) Before Mount Everest was discovered, what was the highest mountain in the world?

7) The day before yesterday, Amy was 7 years old. Next year, she'll be 10. How is this possible?

8) The one who made it didn't want it. The one who bought it didn't need it. The one who used it never saw it. What is it?

ANSWERS ON PAGE 134

NUMBER SNAKE

As you know, Christopher Bent only became a maths genius after stealing Professor Cortex's brain formula. You will have to solve this test **without** any help. Start at the beginning of the snake and make all the calculations in your head. The test starts . . . NOW!

START WITH 2

ADD 2

ADD 1

DOUBLE IT

ADD 10

TAKE AWAY 5

DOUBLE IT

DIVIDE BY 10

TAKE AWAY 2

FINAL ANSWER

CLASSIFIED

MISSION FILE

Ref: GM451/05/RCKTRDR

BACKGROUND

Professor Cortex decided to take a break from Spy School and try teaching at a normal school, which he enjoyed enormously. He continued to invent new gadgets. While visiting him GM451 discovered some information about her family history and decided to try to find her father in Scotland – without telling the Cooks.

MISSION

With her usual skill as a danger magnet, GM451 stumbled on a secret plot on her way to find her dad. A gang aimed to make the whole country desperate for Jimmy's Tartan Suncream – by causing an ecological catastrophe.

SUMMARY

The Cook children and Professor Cortex set off to find GM451, and got in a very dangerous situation. With the help of her father, Leo, GM451 just managed to foil Jimmy's plans at the last second. Most of the gang were captured, but Jimmy escaped and is still at large.

CONCLUSIONS

GM451 was injured again, and the Cook children were threatened by an armed man. Luckily Leo managed to rescue them. While receiving medical treatment, GM451 discovered why she'd been so hungry and tired during her adventure.

Mission Log Extract

'And away we go,' woofed Lara, standing on her hind legs and giving the saddle a little shove forward. The pet audience applauded as Jake's legs began to pump and he wobbled his way out of the garden gate. The animals rushed out into the cul-de-sac to watch, George taking up the rear. They marvelled as Lara trotted behind Jake for a little while and then held their breath as she let go. The bike wobbled, but Jake stayed aboard as he gathered pace down the hill.

'I'm doing it, Lara!' he yapped. 'But don't let go, will you?'

Lara looked at the assembled crowd and shrugged. *Too late for that*, she thought.

'How do I stop again?' came a rather worried woof.

'The brakes,' barked Lara from afar. 'Pull the lever and you'll stop.'

At this point the assembled team learnt a valuable lesson. 'Never look backwards when you're riding a bike,' Lara explained as Jake's nose pointed towards them. 'Otherwise you'll lose your balance.'

Spy Dog Rocket Rider

Ben was complaining to a friend. 'My dog will chase anyone on a bicycle.'

'That must be annoying.'

'It is. If she keeps it up I'll have to stop her riding that bike.'

What's the hardest part of learning to ride a bike? The pavement.

Lara was riding her bike along a country lane when a cyclist coming the other way shouted 'Pig! Pig!'

Lara thought that was very rude, and was really angry – until she went round the next corner and ran into a pig.

Dad was riding his bike to work when he accidentally ran into a pedestrian and knocked him down. 'Wow, you were lucky!' he laughs.

'What do you mean?' said the man. 'That really hurt!'

'Yeah, but I usually drive to work.'

Why can't a bicycle stand up on its own?
Because it's two-tyred.

Mum paid for lessons to learn how to ride a bike, but she could only afford half the lessons.

She can only ride a unicycle.

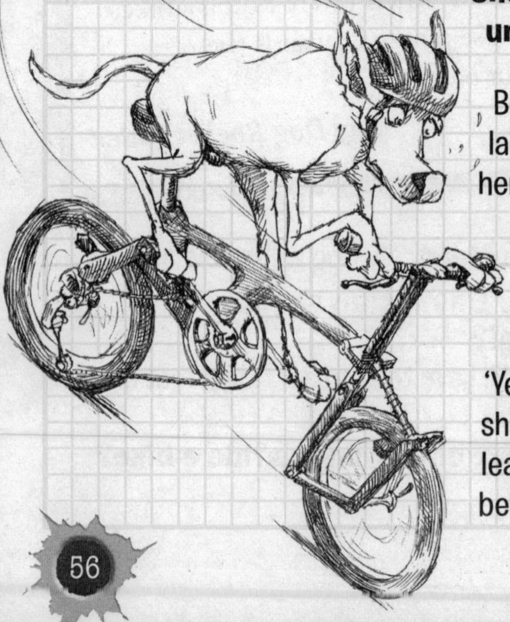

Ben swerved round an old lady on his bike and gave her a fright.

'You hooligan!' she yelled. 'Don't you know how to ride a bike?'

'Yes,' called Ben over his shoulder. 'But I haven't learnt how to ring the bell yet.'

PERSONAL FILE

Ref: GM451/GDYNML001

Classification: Canine Support

Name: Potter

Appearance: shaggy black pedigree dog

Personality: Intelligent, sympathetic and supportive, good all-round skills. Looks up to GM451.

History: GM451 considers Potter her second-in-command at the animal neighbourhood watch, and tells him everything. They have become very close.

How do you catch a runaway dog?
Hide behind a bush and make a noise like a bone.

Which is the cleanest breed of dog?
The shampoodle.

When a big Rottweiler comes to visit, where does he sit?
Anywhere he wants.

What did the hungry Dalmatian say when he finally got a big meal?
'That hit the spots!'

What do dogs have that no other animal has?
Puppies.

What do you get if you cross a cocker spaniel, a poodle and a rooster?
'Cockerpoodledoo!'

I finally managed to make my dog stop barking in the front garden - I put her in the back garden instead.

Every time the doorbell rings, my dog runs to the corner of the room.
He's a boxer.

What has 200 eyes and 400 legs?
One hundred dogs.

CORTEX BRAINDUMP 0009

PROBLEM:
George the tortoise is too slow to join in with Lara's neighbourhood watch.

SOLUTION:
A little skateboard he can whizz about on.

NEW PROBLEM:
His little legs get tired, especially going uphill.

NEW SOLUTION:
Attach a small rocket to the skateboard! That'll be fine, perfectly safe.

Mission Log Extract

'I've found out about my family,' she woofed ever so quietly in the dark. There was silence, except for the humming of the fridge.

'I bet they're really special dogs,' replied Potter eventually. 'Which explains why you're so amazing.'

'My grandmother was certainly very special,' agreed Lara. She told Potter everything that was in Mr Jetski's diary. How she was related to Laika, the first animal in space. 'She was my great-grandmother.' About how Laika was identified as superintelligent, which was why she was chosen for the mission. And how the Russians had kept Laika's story a secret before eventually reporting that she'd died. 'But she didn't die in space,' explained Lara. 'The diary says she landed safely. Splashed down in the ocean. The Russian government were very secretive because they didn't want anyone else to get their hands on this superdog.' Lara knew the diary off by heart. 'And a Russian astronaut, Oleg Jetski, has kept the line of dogs going through a special breeding programme.'

Spy Dog Rocket Rider

Where do astronauts keep their sandwiches?
In a launchbox.

How does an astronaut get her baby to sleep?
Rocket.

How did the rocket lose its job?
It got fired.

Two astronauts found a party on the moon, but they didn't stay very long. There was no atmosphere.

How do they pass the time on trips to the moon?
By playing astronauts and crosses.

Which astronaut wears the biggest helmet?
The one with the biggest head.

What did the astronaut cook for lunch?
An unidentified frying object.

Where do astronauts leave their rockets?
At a parking meteor.

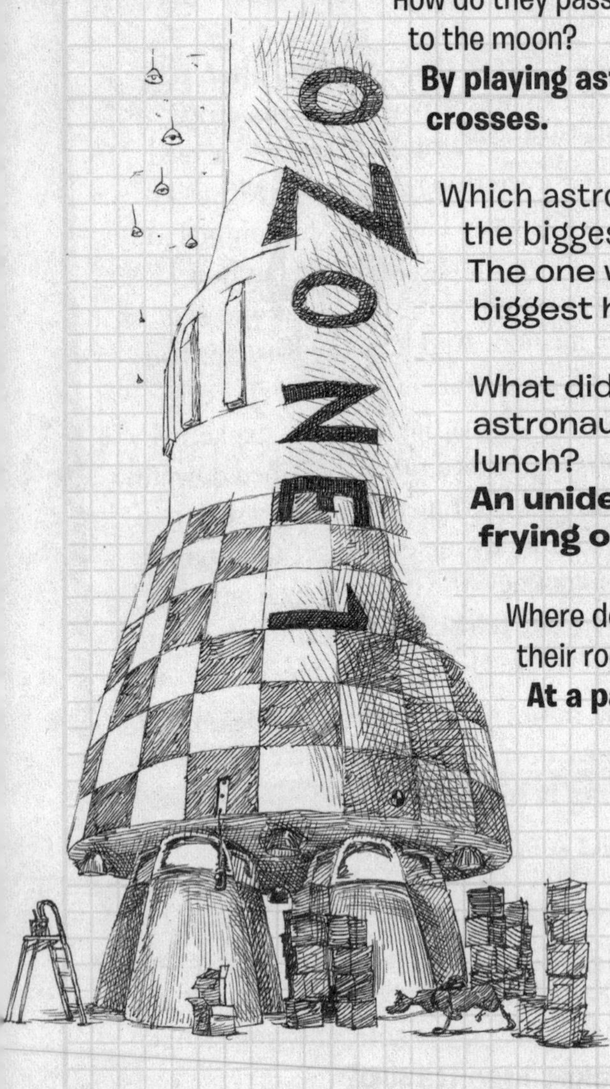

PERSONAL FILE

Ref: GM451/BDY0007

Classification: Villain

Name: Jimmy – surname unknown

Appearance: Appears to be a slim, attractive thirty-year-old with blue eyes and black hair. May be wearing make-up?

Personality: Extremely focused on becoming very rich by any means. Prepared to suffer to get what he wants. No concern for others or the planet.

History: Unknown. Appeared as if from nowhere on TV, advertising his Tartan Suncream – in the middle of

Jimmy claims his suncream is new and improved. But if it's new, how can it be improved? And if it's improved, how can it be new?

Jimmy woke up, looked in the mirror and saw red.
Someone had coloured his face with felt-tip.

Dad fell asleep while watching football on TV. Mum found him next morning still lying on the sofa, and woke him up with a shake. 'Come on, it's ten to nine!'

'Wow, really?' yelled Dad. 'Who's winning?'

Jimmy was starting to experience the three signs of getting older. The first was memory loss, the second was losing his hair and the third was memory loss.

What do refuse workers use to see where the rubbish is?
Bin-oculars.

Jimmy went to get his eyes tested, and guess who he bumped into . . .
Everyone.

Jimmy needed glasses because he was seeing spots. They made a great difference – when he wore them, the spots were much sharper.

CORTEX BRAINDUMP 0010

PROBLEM:
Cleaning pets is frustrating for the owner and stressful for the pet.

SOLUTION:
The Pet-o-Matic, an automated animal cleaner.

NEW PROBLEM:
Owners get jealous that their pets get cleaner faster than they do.

NEW SOLUTION:
The People-o-Matic . . . not sure if it would work, though!

Mission Log Extract

Jimmy had a plan that was pure evil. He went to the bathroom and looked in the mirror. He saw a handsome man, about thirty years old, with sparkling blue eyes and a mop of black hair. 'See you later, young Jimmy.' He reached up and grabbed a flap of skin under his skin. There was a squelching sound as he started to peel off his face. Jimmy had spent ten years experimenting with the sun's radiation and it had shrivelled his skin so he looked as if he'd spent a whole day in the swimming pool. Except Jimmy's wrinkles were deep and sore.

Next came the hair, and his contact lenses came out last. Jimmy fixed his thick-rimmed spectacles on to his face and looked in the mirror again. 'Howdy, old Jimmy.' Thirty had become a hundred and thirty! He'd got used to the red eyes, wrinkly face and burnt scalp. It was the price he'd paid for perfecting his suncream formula.

Spy Dog Rocket Rider

What did the pig on the sunny beach say?
'Phew, I'm bacon!'

Sophie and the boys arrived in Scotland on a miserable, cold, rainy day. 'Does the sun ever shine here?' she asked a local boy.

'I don't know,' he replied. 'I'm only six.'

Some people can tell the time by looking at the sun. But I've never been able to make out the numbers.

Jimmy stayed up all night once, wondering where the sun went.
Eventually it dawned on him.

Ben: 'They're going to send a space mission to the sun.'
Sophie: 'Won't that be dangerously hot?'
Ben: 'I expect they'll land at night.'

Why is a woman wearing sunglasses like a bad teacher?
She keeps her pupils in the dark.

Reading a really good book while sunbathing can make you well-red.

'Wow, the sun's really hot today!'
'Well, don't touch it then.'

Ollie talks so much that when he goes on holiday he has to put suncream on his tongue.

STEP ON NO PETS

This could be the motto of Lara's neighbourhood watch. But it's also a *palindrome* – a sentence that reads the same backwards. Here are a few more that Ben and Sophie came up with:

LIVE NOT ON EVIL

NEVER ODD OR EVEN

PULL UP IF I PULL UP

A NUT FOR A JAR OF TUNA

TOO HOT TO HOOT

RACE FAST, SAFE CAR

SO MANY DYNAMOS

WAS IT A CAR OR A BAT I SAW?

TODD ERASES A RED DOT

BORROW OR ROB?

TOO BAD I HID A BOOT

CIGAR? TOSS IT IN A CAN, IT IS SO TRAGIC

DID I DRAW DELLA TOO TALL,
EDWARD? I DID

Can you spot which one of these **isn't** a palindrome?
How can you change it to make it work?

ANSWERS ON PAGE 135

Brain XLR8R Test 04

Keep paying attention – these questions are only easy if you know what you're doing.

1) There's a word that is wrong if you pronounce it right, and right if you pronounce it wrong. What is the word?

2) You're running in a race when you overtake the person in second place. What position are you in now?

3) How many things can you name that you wear on your feet, beginning with the letter S? Can you manage ten?

4) You're in a remote cabin in total darkness, with only one match left to light a candle, a lamp, the stove and the fire. Which do you light first?

5) What is so fragile that it will break if you even say its name?

6) A farmer left for market on Wednesday. It took him two whole days to walk there; he stayed for one day and bought a horse. He rode home the next day and got back on Friday. How?

7) Who's bigger – Mr Bigger, Mrs Bigger or their baby?

8) A businessman pushed his car to a hotel and told the hotel owner that he had just become bankrupt. Why?

ANSWERS ON PAGE 135

CLASSIFIED

MISSION FILE

Ref: GM451/06/ TRSRQST

BACKGROUND

GM451 gave birth to seven puppies. Five went to good homes, but the last two, Star and Spud, stayed with her and the Cooks. She began training them in Spy Dog techniques as soon as they were old enough.

MISSION

This was definitely **not** a Secret Service mission. GM451, the Cook children and the puppies went to stay with a relative while Mrs Cook recovered from an injury. While there, the puppies displayed the same ability to find trouble as their mother. They discovered that a neighbour was searching for hidden treasure. Art Burlington had teamed up with the local police constable, PC Winkle, and was desperate to get hold of the lost gold.

Aggressive and dangerous

SUMMARY

The puppies showed great skill and intelligence, and helped their mother capture the villains. They also discovered where the treasure had been hidden for 200 years. Spud received a bullet-hole in his ear – just like his mother.

CONCLUSIONS

Since they seemed to have the same potential as GM451, who was getting older and had been injured several times, it was decided to enrol SPUD (Super Performing Undercover Dog) and STAR (Special Tactics and Rescue) into the Secret Service.

How can you tell if you're a pirate?
If you aargh, you are.

What is a big strong pirate with a wooden leg frightened of?
Nothing - except woodworm.

What was the ghost pirate called?
Captain Hooo-wooo-k.

What stories did the pirate captain tell his children?
Ferry tales.

What has eight legs and eight eyes?
Eight pirates.

Why do seagulls fly over the sea?
If they flew over the bay, they'd be bagels.

Mission Log Extract

'As you know, this house is called Smugglers' Cottage,' began Aunt Aggie. 'So called because it was famous as a hideout for smugglers and pirates in the eighteenth century.'

Spud and Star cocked their heads to one side, hanging on every word.

Ollie's mouth fell open. 'Like in *Pirates of the Caribbean?*' he asked.

'A bit,' nodded Aunt Aggie. 'Chatterton Castle, which you drove past on the way here, was once owned by a wealthy family who were con artists, crooks and thieves. They worked with the smugglers to lure ships on to the rocks below this house.' Aunt Aggie paused for effect. They could all hear the wind howling and the distant crash of sea on the rocks.

Ollie gulped and Star and Spud huddled even closer.

'Legend has it that many men died on nights like this. The smugglers waved lights from the cliffs and the ships thought it was the signal for safety. But instead their ships were smashed into a thousand pieces.'

Spy Pups Treasure Quest

When does a pirate stand at the very back end of his ship?
When he's being stern.

What do you say to a pirate with one leg?
'Hop aboard, matey!'

Ref: GM451/
FMLY001/2/6

Classification: Approved Associates

Names: Mr and Mrs Cook, and Gran. We really must find out their first names.

Appearance: Oh, you know. Parents. A granny. Sweet, really. Why haven't we got any photos?

Personality: Very caring and kind, but often worried about the adventures the Cook children end up getting involved in.

History: After a terrible telling-off from Mrs Cook, the Secret Service are under strict orders to keep the younger Cooks safe at all times. Sadly GM451 and her pups continue to disrupt our best efforts. Gran, on the other hand, knows nothing about GM451's adventures, and still thinks 'Lara' is a soppy, ugly mutt.

Mum went to collect the post from the doormat, but called out for help.

'What's the matter?' called Dad.

'There's a letter for me marked "Do Not Bend",' wailed Mum.

'So what?' said Dad.

'Well, how am I going to pick it up?'

Mum sent Dad to the shops. 'Could you get a carton of milk? And if they've got eggs, get six.'

Dad came back with six cartons of milk, and Mum went mad. 'What on earth did you get all that milk for?'

'Because they had eggs.'

Dad asked Mum what she wanted for Valentine's Day.

'Not much,' she replied. 'Some chocolate and a nice little surprise would be lovely.'

So he gave her a Kinder Egg.

Dad went to a shoe shop to try on some new shoes. 'How do they feel?' asked the assistant.

'The left one's a bit tight,' replied Dad.

The assistant looked at Dad's feet, and realized what was wrong. 'Sir, you need to try it with the tongue out.'

Dad looked at her. 'Thorry, it thtill feelth a bit tighth.'

CORTEX BRAINDUMP 0011

PROBLEM:

Dogs can't see in the dark like cats.

SOLUTION:

Torches on helmets!

NEW PROBLEM:

Small dogs not strong enough to carry all the batteries needed to power the torches.

NEW SOLUTION:

Tap into a dog's natural energy somehow – would poo power work?

Mission Log Extract

The children turned to go as two men approached from the village. One was a policeman in a dark blue uniform. The other was speaking very loudly in an American accent. Sophie winced at his clothing choice of bright pink trousers and lime green jumper.

'What are you kids doing up here?' yelled the American as he came towards them. 'Can't you see it's private?'

'His voice is as loud as his clothes,' whispered Sophie.

'Er, we did see the signs,' admitted Ben, 'but we thought it was worth asking. Our aunt says there's old treasure hidden in this area and we just wanted to have a look around, if that's OK?'

As the two men stalked up to the children, Ollie jumped as he recognized the policeman. His big nose was unmistakeable – it was the man from his bedroom the night before, he was sure!

Spy Pups Treasure Quest

PC Winkle was questioning a suspect in a burglary.

'Where were you between four and six?' he demanded.

'Infant school,' replied the suspect.

Aunt Aggie went into the police station with a dead fox. 'I found this by the side of the road,' she told PC Winkle.

'I'll take your details,' said PC Winkle, 'and if no one claims it in three months, you can keep it.'

PC Winkle was on patrol when he saw a woman driving and knitting at the same time.

'Hey, you! Pull over!' he shouted.

'No, a pair of socks,' she yelled back as she drove past him.

What do you call a flying policeman?
A heli-copper.

PC Winkle caught two men stealing a flat car battery and a firework.
He charged one of them and let the other one off.

PC Winkle was ordered to investigate the theft of ten thousand bars of soap.
Apparently the thieves made a clean getaway.

How do you join the police force?
With lots of handcuffs.

PERSONAL FILE

Ref: GM451/BDY0008

Classification: Villain

Name: Art Burlington

Appearance: Short, fat and loud – both in voice and clothing

Personality: Rude and unpleasant

History: Ran away from New York, where we suspect he had a criminal record. Bought Chatterton Castle when he heard about the hidden gold, but was running out of places to search when the Spy Pups arrived.

Art was ordering in the castle cafe. 'I wanna cuppa coffee, no milk.'

The waitress came back five minutes later. 'I'm afraid we've just run out of milk; would you like your coffee without cream instead?'

Why did the New Yorker cross the road?
'Hey – it ain't none o' ya business, buddy!'

Art ordered some lunch. 'Gimme two bacon double cheeseburgers, with extra cheese, two large portions of fries . . . and a **diet** cola.'

Art ordered a steak and the waiter came back holding the steak down with his thumb.

'Hey, what are you doin'? Take ya dirty fingers off my food!' yelled Art.

'What,' said the waiter, 'and drop it on the floor again?'

Art noticed a fly in his coffee. He scooped it out on a spoon, held it by the wings over his cup and snarled, 'Spit it out, you thief!'

How many tourists does it take to change a light bulb?

Nine. Three to work out how to buy a replacement with the weird local currency, two to talk about how 'funny-looking' light bulbs are here, one to hire a local guy to change the bulb, two to take photos all the time and one to buy postcards of light bulbs in case the photos don't come out.

CORTEX BRAINDUMP 0012

PROBLEM:
Occasionally dogs need to hide explosives.

SOLUTION:
Exploding bones! No one suspects a dog carrying a bone.

NEW PROBLEM:
Other dogs steal the bones if they get left anywhere.

NEW SOLUTION:
Exploding dog biscuits? No, same problem. Exploding poos? I seem to be running out of ideas . . .

Where do ghosts go on holiday?
The Isle of Fright . . . they fly there with British Scareways.

How can you tell if a ghost is flat?
Use a spirit level.

What's a ghost's favourite food?
I-scream.

Why do ghosts make bad magicians?
You can see right through their tricks.

When do ghosts usually appear?
Right before someone screams.

What should you say when you meet a ghost?
'How do you boo?'

What did the dragon say when he saw a knight wearing armour?
'Oh no, not tinned food again.'

Mission Log Extract

The children and Lara sat down and peered at the menu. The waiter arrived and Ben ordered four hot chocolates. The man looked surprised. 'But there are only three of you,' he said.

Lara wagged hard and winked at the man. *Think again,* she panted. *I'm not missing out.*

'Um, I really like hot chocolate,' said Sophie, giving him her sweetest smile.

The children looked around at the cafe as they waited. There were all sorts of ancient pictures on the walls. 'Lots of paintings of ships,' pointed Sophie. 'On the high seas. I bet one of those is the galleon that had the gold.'

'And portraits like in haunted houses,' noted Ollie. 'They might be the smugglers and pirates.'

'And check out that suit of armour,' said Sophie. 'You'd hardly be able to walk if you wore that!'

Spy Pups Treasure Quest

What was Camelot famous for?
The exciting knight life.

A knight was killed in battle and buried in his armour. What did they write on his gravestone?
'Rust in peace.'

What did King Arthur say when he wanted everyone sitting at the Round Table to stand up and change places?
'Time for the knight shift.'

Treasure Test

Look at the map. Start from the square at the top left – A1 – and follow the instructions to find where the treasure is hidden.

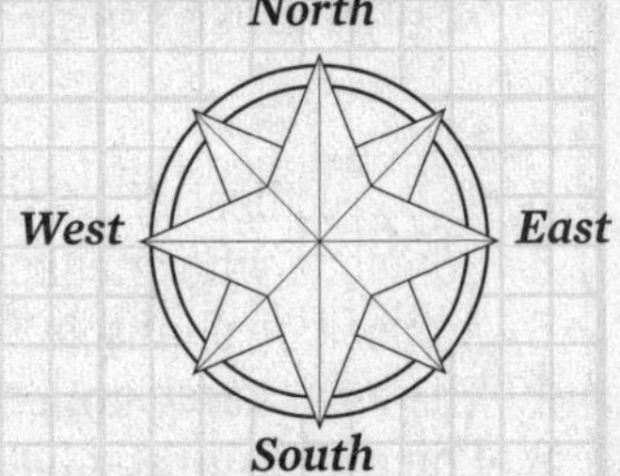

Go east seven squares, south six squares, west one square, north two squares, west one square, south one square and west three squares. Dig in the square directly to the north-east.

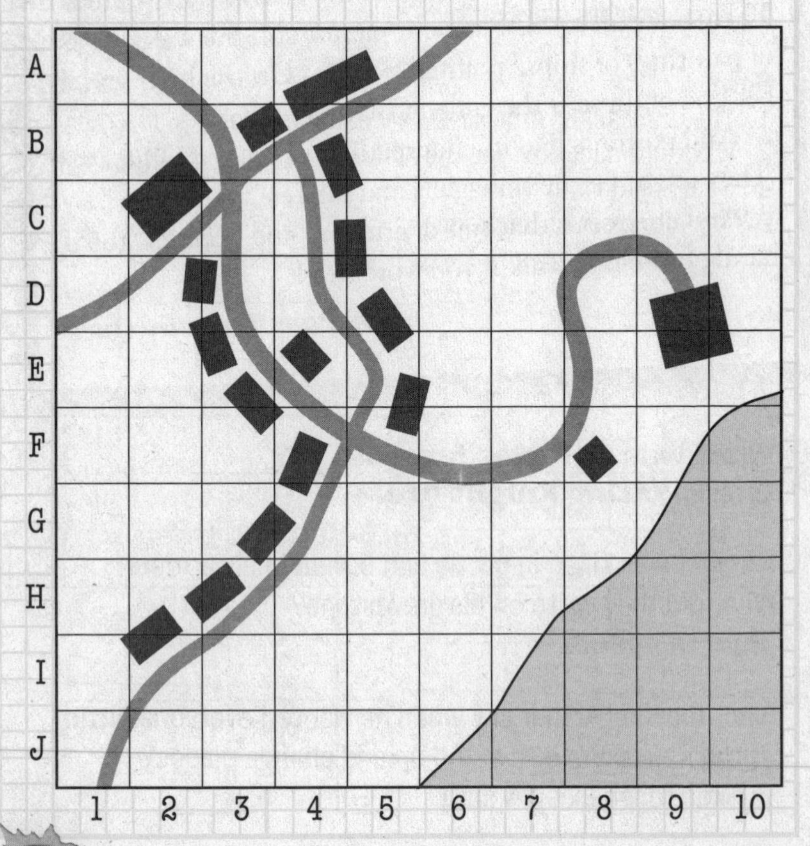

Canine Crossword

GM451 likes to settle down with a custard cream and a crossword, glasses perched on the end of her nose. Time to copy her – but you'll have to fetch your own biscuit.

Across

3 The greediest of Lara's puppies
5 Someone who sneaks things ashore
6 A spook or phantom
7 The local nasty policeman
8 Someone who steals things at sea
10 What knights wore suits of

Down

1 The unpleasant American searching for gold
2 Where he's looking for the gold
4 Ben, Sophie and Ollie's aunt
9 The cleverest of Lara's puppies

ANSWERS ON PAGE 135

CLASSIFIED

MISSION FILE

Ref: GM451/07/PRSNBRK

BACKGROUND

Although he was behind bars in a maximum-security prison, Mr Big continued to threaten the life of GM451. He sent her some poisoned custard creams for her birthday and, foolishly, she scoffed the lot. *Big mistake!*

MISSION

GM451 became extremely ill. Professor Cortex and the Spy Pups agreed to break Mr Big out of prison, as he demanded, in the hope that he would give them the antidote.

Even bigger mistake!

SUMMARY

It was very close – the antidote was given to GM451, but she had literally minutes left to live. *She was incredibly lucky*

CONCLUSIONS

Ben and the pups were in grave danger. They also caused a considerable amount of damage to property, which we had to pay for. Professor Cortex got in a lot of trouble with the Secret Service. Big's present location remains unknown.

Mission Log Extract

Mrs Cook put the bone-shaped cake on to the coffee table and Lara beckoned to her puppies. 'Come on then, you two,' she woofed. 'Help me blow out the candles and then we can open some pressies.'

Ben, the eldest of the Cook children, photographed the dogs as they took deep breaths and blew out the candles in one go. Everyone cheered and Mrs Cook cut slices for everyone. Spud wolfed his down and came back for more, his tail almost wagging him off his feet.

Lara raised an eyebrow as she passed a small second helping to him. *His waistline isn't quite in keeping with a Spy Dog*, she thought. *But I'm sure it's just puppy fat*.

'Are you going to open your presents now, Lara?' asked Ollie, the youngest child. 'You've got loads. Especially for a dog.'

Lara eyed the pile of gift-wrapped presents and smiled a doggie smile. Most were in the shape of balls or bones so it was easy to guess what they were.

Spy Pups Prison Break

What do cows play at birthday parties?
Moosical chairs. Right after they've sung 'Happy Birthday to Moo.'

What does Lara always get on her birthday?
Another year older.

Why do we put candles on top of birthday cakes?
It's too tricky to put them on the bottom.

'Mum, do you know what I'm getting you for your birthday? A nice teapot.'

'But, Ollie, I've already got a nice teapot.'

'Not any more, you haven't – I just dropped it.'

Gran had so many candles on her birthday cake last year that everyone got sunburnt. This year we're going to invite the fire brigade, just in case.

What do you give an angry gorilla for his birthday?
I'm not sure, but you'd better hope he likes it.

What does an oyster do on her birthday?
She shellebrates.

Which is the left side of a birthday cake?
The side that hasn't been eaten.

PERSONAL FILE

Ref: GM451/HR002

Classification: Trainee Agent

Name: SPUD

Appearance: Black fur, like his dad. Bullet-hole through one ear, like his mum. Bit podgy for his age.

Personality: Spud loves excitement. Almost fearless – always the first to dive into any dangerous situation. Very fond of his food, which may cause him problems in the future.

History: Spud was trained almost from birth in Spy Dog techniques by GM451, and has received intensive education acceleration from Professor Cortex. He shows great potential – if he can keep his weight down.

Spud fell asleep on a hairdryer.
It really put the wind up him.

What does Spud like to eat when he goes to the cinema?
Pup-corn.

How does Spud know when he needs to lose weight?
When it's raining, but his feet aren't getting wet.

Spud isn't overweight. He's just a bit undertall.

Spud got very excited when he saw a cafe advertising a full chicken dinner for only 20p.
It turned out all you got was a saucer of birdseed.

Spud watched a very interesting TV show about mallards.
It was a duckumentary.

Spud ate a whole bulb of garlic last week.
It made his bark much, much worse than his bite.

CORTEX BRAINDUMP 0013

PROBLEM:
We know where the dogs are, thanks to the GPS transmitters in their collars. But THEY don't know where they are.

SOLUTION:
GPS receiver in a watch.

NEW PROBLEM:
Dogs wearing watches tend to stand out a bit!

NEW SOLUTION:
Match a fur watchstrap to the dog's natural colour and put a flap of fur over the watch face.

Mission Log Extract

Outside, the race was well and truly underway. Grandma Cook was walking up the cul-de-sac as Danny raced by.

'Hello, Danny Boy,' waved the old lady. 'And goodbye again,' she said as her favourite dog blurred past. Then from round the corner came a Rollerblading cat. 'Connie,' she said, dropping her shopping bag, 'is that you?'

'Meeeoooeow,' wailed Connie, unable to stop.

'You do see some amazing things nowadays,' muttered Gran, picking up her basket and setting off again. The old lady hadn't gone three steps before George hurtled round the corner. He'd taken it too fast and was clipping the hedge as he went.

'George?' said Gran, dropping her shopping again. The old lady leapt out of the way as the rocket-propelled reptile whizzed past in a cloud of smoke.

Spy Pups Prison Break

Gran entered a 'Prominent Leg Veins' competition.
She didn't win, but she came varicose.

Gran met a neighbour when she went out for a walk.

'Windy, isn't it?' said Gran.

'No, it's Thursday,' replied the neighbour.

'Ooh, so am I,' said Gran. 'Do you want to come in for a cup of tea?'

Why are Christmas trees like Gran when she's knitting?
They both drop needles.

Ben went to see Gran. 'Can you help me with a jigsaw puzzle, dear?' she asked. 'It's really hard - I can't even find any edge pieces.'

'What's it a puzzle of, Gran?' asked Ben.

'A big chicken eating breakfast,' replied Gran.

'That's not a puzzle, Gran. Now let's go and put the cornflakes back.'

Gran was dreaming someone was shouting 'On your marks, get set, go!' at her.
She woke up with a start.

Gran got a new flat-screen TV. Ben was admiring it, and asked how she changed channels.

'I haven't the remotest idea,' she said.

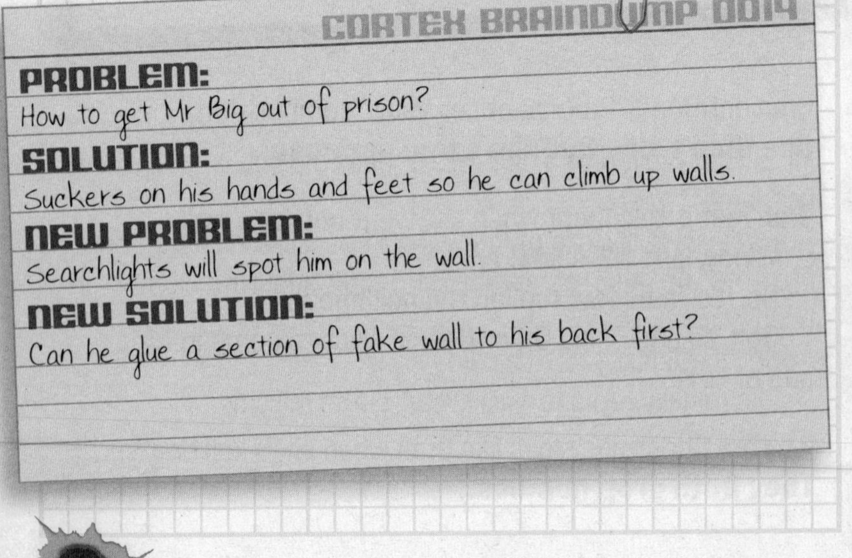

PERSONAL FILE

Ref: GM451/BDY0001/B

Classification: Villain (updated)

Name: Mr Big (first name still unknown)

Appearance: Significantly changed since last entry. He has had plastic surgery at some point and is now tall and slim, with a film star's good looks. The thick glossy hair may not be his own.

Personality: Just as vicious and cruel as always.

History: Luckily, Mr Big is now securely locked up on Hurtmore Island, the most secure prison in the world.

Mr Big got moved to a cell with a really old guy who told him how he got there.

'I was living the life of Riley. I had four cars, a speedboat, ate in all the best restaurants and took beautiful women on holiday six times a year.'

'So what happened?' asked Mr Big.

'Riley finally reported his credit cards missing.'

On his first day at Hurtmore Island, Mr Big hears an inmate yell out, 'Thirty-two.'

Everybody in the cell block starts laughing.

Another inmate yells out, 'Fifty-seven.' Again, everybody laughs.

Mr Big asks his cellmate why everybody's laughing.

The cellmate explains, 'We've been in here so long, that we all know everybody's jokes. To save time we've numbered them.'

Mr Big thinks for a moment and then yells out, 'Forty-three.' Nobody laughs. He tries again, louder: 'Forty-three!' Again, nobody laughs. Mr Big asks his cellmate, 'What happened? Why isn't anybody laughing?'

His cellmate replied, 'You told it wrong.'

A prisoner visited the hospital doctor. 'Listen, you said you were going to help me escape. But all you've done is operate on me - so far you've taken out my tonsils, spleen, one kidney and my appendix.'

'I am getting you out of prison,' replied the doctor. 'Bit by bit.'

Mr Big asked a prisoner what he was in for.

'Doing my Christmas shopping early,' said the man.

'That doesn't sound particularly criminal,' said Mr Big.

'It is if the shops haven't opened yet.'

Mission Log Extract

Ben was doing well. He'd navigated a field of cows and cleared two ditches. The tractor was muddied and battered but was still going strong.

Star used her doggie watch to point out the directions. 'Five miles to go,' she yapped. 'That-a-way!'

The huge tyres meant that fields were no trouble at all, even muddy ones. Hedges could easily be breached and streams crossed. The trio had found their way on to a country lane and were bouncing along as fast as the tractor would take them. Ben hit the brakes hard and the tractor stalled at a crossroads. He recognized the name of one of the towns. 'Not too far now!' he yelled, as he turned the key and the engine roared into life again.

The road widened as they approached the town. As they stopped at some traffic lights, they pulled up alongside Ben's head teacher, Mr Bell. There weren't many tractors in town. The man glanced up and the puppies waved.

'Hi there,' beamed Spud.

'We're just on a bit of an adventure,' waved his sister. 'We're Spy Pups, see. And this is a mission.'

Spy Pups Prison Break

What kind of bird lays electric eggs?
A battery hen.

How do you fit more pigs on our farm?
Build a sty-scraper.

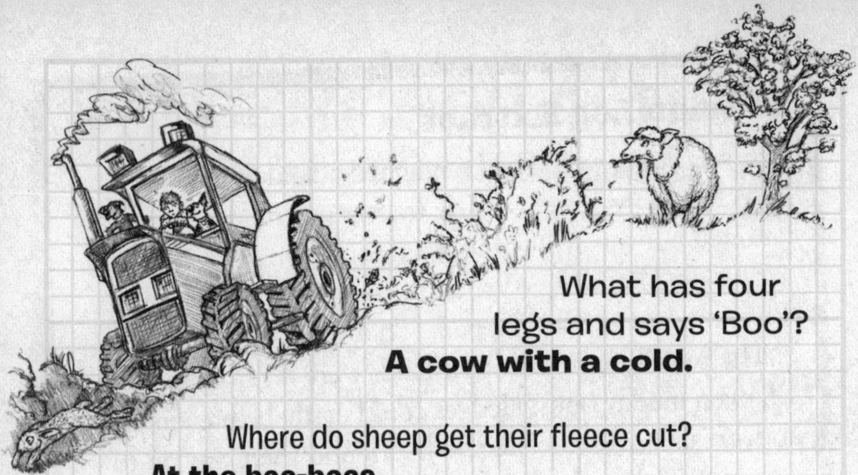

What has four legs and says 'Boo'?
A cow with a cold.

Where do sheep get their fleece cut?
At the baa-baas.

What do you get if you cross a cow with a camel?
Lumpy milkshakes.

What does a polite sheep say as she leaves the field?
'After ewe.'

Why did the pony keep coughing?
Because she was a little horse. (So the vet gave her some cough stirrup.)

Two sheep were standing in a field.
'Baaa,' says one.
'Oh, bother,' says the other. 'I was just about to say that.'

What's the difference between a duck and a cow?
They can both swim, apart from the cow.

A farmer took his cows to market every Wednesday, but he never sold a single one. After six months, someone told him market day was Saturday.

Brain XLR8R Test 05

By now you should be much cleverer than when you started. Let's find out.

1) What is it that you sit on, sleep in and brush your teeth with?

2) Ben threw a ball as hard as he could. It didn't hit anything or bounce off anything, and it wasn't fixed to anything – yet it came straight back to him. How?

3) A farmer told his two sons to race their horses to a far-off town. The son whose horse got there ***last*** would inherit the farm. Confused, the sons rode off as slowly as possible. After a few days, they'd given up riding when they met a wise woman, who gave them some advice. As soon as she finished speaking, the sons jumped back on the horses and rode off as fast as possible. What did the woman say?

4) A friend comes out of the library and tells you she's hidden ten pounds in between pages 75 and 76 of a book. Should you go and look for it?

5) You have six glasses in a row. The three on the left are full of juice, the three on the right are empty. How can you move only one glass, yet arrange them so that empty and full glasses alternate?

6) You throw away the outside, then cook the inside. Then you eat the outside, and throw away the inside. What have you eaten?

7) It lives without a body, hears without ears, speaks without a mouth, and is born and dies in the air. What is it?

8) What goes round and round the wood, but never goes into the wood?

ANSWERS ON PAGE 135

SPOT THE SHADOW

Here's Lara in full action mode – but only one of these shadows is her real one. Can you spot it?

ANSWER ON PAGE 136

~~CLASSIFIED~~

MISSION FILE

Ref: GM451/08/CRCSCT

BACKGROUND

Jewellery, especially diamonds, were being stolen all over the country. We suspected Clarissa White was behind the thefts, and that a travelling circus was involved, but couldn't work out how the burglars were getting in – they left no evidence at all.

White's a nasty piece of work

MISSION

The pups were asked to work at the circus, and try to find out what was going on. They realized some of the performers were committing the burglaries during the show, and set off in pursuit.

Training came in handy here

SUMMARY

Yet again, the Cook children ended up being dragged into a dangerous situation. Fierce animals threatened the public. Circus vehicles were driven recklessly. And the criminals were all captured.

Ice creams got eaten, too

CONCLUSIONS

To be honest, the puppies weren't really responsible for getting the children into trouble – they did that all on their own. Perhaps we need to train them as well as the puppies.

Mission Log Extract

'This is Tony Jewell. Owner, ringmaster and, by all accounts, dreadful chap,' said Professor Cortex. 'Shouts a lot. Bullies people. Nasty man. And yes, Oliver, extraordinary eyebrows. But that doesn't make him a criminal.'

Spud let out a low growl. 'I don't like him. Not if he shouts at people.'

'And here's his wife, Jennifer Jewell. Lovely lady. From what we can make out, she's the opposite of her husband. And here are a few of the performers and animals,' continued the professor, clicking rapidly through a few slides.

Lara, the pups and the children gasped at some of the pictures.

'A bearded lady!' woofed Star, amazed.

Ollie nearly fell off his seat when he saw the trapeze artist. 'We definitely need to get involved with this one,' he said. 'It'd be *so* exciting to visit the circus.'

'But the elephant and lions are not so exciting,' yapped Spud. 'That's cruel!'

'It's more than *visiting*,' noted the professor. 'I want the puppies to *infiltrate* the circus.'

'What's *infiltrate*?' asked Ollie.

'Spy on!' said Ben, his eyes shining.

Spy Pups Circus Act

Why do monkeys have big nostrils?
Because they've got big fingers.

What's the name of that really bad lion tamer?
Claude Bottom.

What do you call a lion with toothache?
Rory.

Dad was walking through town when a crowd of people ran towards him. 'Look out!' shouted one of them. 'A lion has escaped from the circus!'

'Which way is it heading?' said Dad, panicking.
'Well, we're not running towards it!'

How do you make instant elephant?
Open the packet, add water and run.

What cheers up a sick elephant?
A Get Wellephant card.

Why don't elephants ride bicycles?
Because they don't have any thumbs to ring the bell with.

How do monkeys make toast?
They put some bread under the gorilla.

PERSONAL FILE

Ref: GM451/HR003

Classification: Trainee Agent

Name: STAR

Appearance: White with black spots, and one ear sticking up – just like her mum, GM451.

Personality: Extremely intelligent – Star can even speak Siamese cat.

History: Star and her brother Spud have proved to be adequate replacements for GM451, who has scaled down her Spy Dog activities to take care of her family.

Dad was very impressed when Star began bringing him the newspaper every morning. Then he realized they didn't get any papers delivered.

What's black and white and red all over?
Star when she's embarrassed.

Why did Star chase her tail?
She was trying to make both ends meet.

Why does Star wag her tail?
Because no one else will do it for her.

Ben bought a dog whistle for Spud and Star, but it didn't really work. Star only learnt one tune and Spud just dribbled.

Star didn't think she could sleep on the washing line.
But she soon dropped off.

CORTEX BRAINDUMP 0015

PROBLEM:
Getting criminals to admit to their crimes.

SOLUTION:
Some kind of truth drug, delivered in a small dart.

NEW PROBLEM:
While testing it on myself, I was far too honest in describing some of my colleagues.

NEW SOLUTION:
Buy lots of biscuits for the office.

Which circus act can see in the dark?
The acro-bats.

A policeman stopped a clown with a desk on his back, a telephone in one hand and a waste-paper basket in the other. 'I'm sorry,' said the policeman, 'but I can't allow you to impersonate an office, sir.'

Why did the clown put birdseed in the garden?
He wanted to grow some birds.

Why did the clown put his cake in the freezer?
He wanted to ice it.

Why did the clown cross the road?
To fetch his rubber chicken.

What's the red stuff between an elephant's toes?
Slow clowns.

Mission Log Extract

There's no way, Star thought as he crouched in the very small box. *I mean, the box is tiny and he's tall. He's defying the laws of physics!*

The rubber man shuffled himself lower. He bent double. *Almost triple!*

Finally, he lowered his head and his assistant flipped the lid shut.

Now that's quite a trick! marvelled Star, clapping her paws together in admiration. *Squeezing into tight places like that would be perfect for a burglar*, she noted.

After that, the Spy Pup lingered near the clowns as they perfected their routine.

What a cool car, she thought as they drove it into the big top in readiness for the evening's show. It was like a mini fire engine with a ladder on the back, but open-topped so the clowns could jump in and out as well as throw things at the crowd. It was mayhem. Star watched as the car drove round the circus ring with a clown hanging off the ladder. Star decided she'd like to train to become a clown. *It looks like such great fun!*

Spy Pups Circus Act

Why did the lion stop eating the clown after one bite?
Because he tasted funny.

Why did the clown wear such loud socks?
To stop his feet falling asleep.

Clarissa's cat caught a duck and ate it all.
Which made her a duck-filled fatty-puss.

What's her cat's favourite colour?
Purrrrr-ple.

Clarissa would never want to be queen.
She couldn't bear to move to a smaller house.

Clarissa was bored one weekend so she wandered round the shops, just window-shopping. She bought thirty windows.

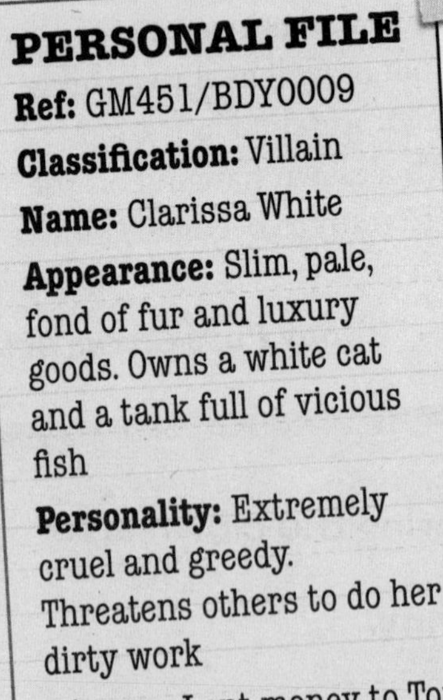

PERSONAL FILE

Ref: GM451/BDY0009

Classification: Villain

Name: Clarissa White

Appearance: Slim, pale, fond of fur and luxury goods. Owns a white cat and a tank full of vicious fish

Personality: Extremely cruel and greedy. Threatens others to do her dirty work

History: Lent money to Tony Jewell, circus owner, then forced him to steal gems to pay her back.

CORTEX BRAINDUMP 0016

PROBLEM:

Disabling the big aggressive bodyguards that baddies seem to have near them.

SOLUTION:

A memory-loss drug that will make them forget their violent skills.

NEW PROBLEM:

I'm sure I tested this on someone, but I can't remember who.

NEW SOLUTION:

I need to work out an antidote and give it to everyone!

How many piranhas can Clarissa put in an empty fish tank?

One - then the tank isn't empty.

Spud got quite worried when Lara showed him an ice-cream van in the park.
He thought it was going to melt.

Mission Log Extract

Ben caught on. 'Prof,' he said, 'are you driving or me?'

Professor Cortex shook his head in disbelief. 'You can't drive, Benjamin,' he spluttered. 'You're only twelve and your mother would never forgive me.'

'So you'll have to do it then, Prof,' yelled Ben, grabbing the man's hand and pulling him towards the van. 'And quick, before Mum comes outside!'

Star made room in the front seat. The scientist plonked himself down and familiarized himself with the controls. 'Seems simple enough,' he said. 'Off we go.'

The ice-cream van juddered away. Ben, Sophie and Star sat up front with the professor. Ollie and Spud were in the back, helping themselves to ice creams. Spud was in doggie heaven. He'd found the Flakes and was already on his fourth 99.

Spy Pups need to keep their energy up! he thought.

The ice-cream van bounced across the grass and on to the tarmac. The professor hit a few switches, looking for the lights. The road came into view. One of the switches started the ice-cream van tune and off they sped in hot pursuit to the accompaniment of 'How Much is that Doggie in the Window?'.

Spy Pups Circus Act

What's a lion's favourite ice cream?
Roar-sberry ripple.

What does a cat like to have when it's hot?
A mice-cream cone.

Why did the ice-cream seller go on holiday?
He wanted to get a-wafer a bit.

'I'd like a small cornet, please, with a Flake and strawberry sauce.'

'OK – hundreds and thousands?'

'No, just the one, thanks.'

'I'd like a cornet with a Flake – a 99, please.'
'I don't think I can fit more than five or six in there, I'm afraid.'

Brain XLR8R Test 06

The final instalment. If these aren't easy, you need to see Professor Cortex for some of his special pills.

1) Poke your fingers in my eyes and I will open my jaws wide. I love to eat paper, cloth and string. What am I?

2) I have a little house in which I live all alone. My house has no doors or windows, and when I want to go out I have to break through the wall. Who am I?

3) What happens twice in a week, and once in a year, but never in a day?

4) What is half of 2 + 2?

5) Your mother's brother's only brother-in-law is asleep on your couch. Who is the sleepyhead?

6) Who can shave 25 times a day and still have a beard?

7) It's better than the best, worse than the worst; the poor have it, and the rich want it; and if you eat it, you'll die. What is it?

8) This is an unusual paragraph. I'm curious how quickly you can find out what is so unusual about it. It looks so plain, you would think nothing was wrong with it. In fact, nothing is wrong with it! It is unusual, though. Study it, and think about it, but you still may not find anything odd. But if you work at it a bit, you might find out what is unusual about this paragraph.

ANSWERS PAGE 136

Here's a very recent addition to the GM451 Files – most agents won't have seen it. The Spy Pups used all their training to prevent a royal disaster.

UNFILED

Mission Log

By Royal Command

The high-speed train whistled towards London. The children were looking forward to their day out. Ben was lost in an iPod movie and Ollie was chatting to his sister. 'So, do you actually think we'll see the Queen?' he asked. 'I wonder if she'll remember me?' He beamed, thinking back to a Spy Dog adventure that had begun at the palace.

'Today's not about the Queen,' explained Sophie. 'It's about her grandson. He's getting married, you see.'

'Cool,' purred Ollie. 'To a princess?'

'Well, I suppose she will be after they've tied the knot,' explained his big sister.

'Why's he tying her up?' asked Ollie. 'It sounds cruel. I don't think you should tie princesses up.'

Mum rolled her eyes. 'It's a shame the dogs

couldn't come,' she said, changing the subject, 'but they're not allowed on trains. And they'd probably get bored waiting for the bride and groom to go by.'

'Plus,' added Dad, 'there's going to be a huge fireworks display. The pups would be scared stiff!'

Ben glanced up from his iPod and caught his sister's eye. They tried to look innocent.

Ben aimed a 'shush' kick at the rucksack that lay under the table. The rucksack fidgeted ever so slightly as the news sunk in. Spud nudged Star. 'We're not just being smuggled to London,' he hissed. 'We're going to see some fireworks!'

Star spied out of Sophie's rucksack, her sensitive nose taking in the smells of the capital city. *So many people*, she thought.

'What's happening, sis?' woofed Spud. 'I can smell food. Are we anywhere near a cafe?'

'Just checking into a hotel,' woofed back his sister. She pricked her ears. 'But the receptionist says we're too early and our room's not ready yet.'

The pups heard Sophie complain that she didn't want to leave her bag but Mum insisted.

'There's no point carrying it around London,' she said, 'so we'll leave the bags at the hotel and collect them when we check in later.'

Spud had the wind knocked out of him as the rucksack was grabbed by a bellboy and thrown into a corner. Now it was his turn to peep. He spied his family disappearing through the hotel's revolving door. The puppy gulped. 'Oh dear,' he woofed as he watched Sophie cast a worried glance backwards. 'Abandoned in London. That wasn't supposed to happen!'

The puppies wriggled to get more comfortable but it was no good. It was a very small bag and a very hot day. 'We have to get out,' said Star. 'I'm thirsty.'

'And I'm hungry,' woofed Spud, 'so I suggest we sneak out, grab a bite, and chill for a bit. The family will be back this afternoon to check in. Then we reveal ourselves. *Ta da!* It'll be too late for them to send us home. They'll have no choice but to take us to the wedding.'

Star wasn't so sure. But she knew she had to get some fresh air. Star was much skinnier than her brother so she was nominated to go first. Her nose peeked out of the rucksack and sniffed. 'Someone coming,' she woofed, retreating into the bag.

Star peeped out. Two glamorous women and a flat-nosed man wandered over to where the puppies were hiding and looked around nervously. Star's spy training alerted her to their nervous body language. She strained to listen, her ears fully extended.

'Let's run through it one last time,' hissed the man. 'Remember, we only have a very small window of opportunity. A royal wedding is the only time the Crown jewels are let out of the Tower of London.' He rubbed his hands in anticipation. 'So today's the day. We're all set for eight p.m. Yvonne, Charlene . . . talk me through it.'

'You're in charge of the fireworks,' explained one of the women. 'So you'll be at the palace, ready to set them off at exactly eight p.m.'

The other lady took over. 'The armoured van will be at the palace at seven p.m. to pick up the jewels that the royals have borrowed for the wedding. We can't steal them at the palace because security will be too tight. And there'll be too many TV cameras. The van arrives back at the Tower just before eight, which is when we strike.'

The first lady took up the story once more. 'The world's attention will be on the palace. And at exactly eight o'clock when the fireworks go off, we'll blow the doors off the van.' She chuckled. 'Caboom! The fireworks will drown out the noise. And we'll have some sparklers of our very own.'

'Priceless ones,' growled flat-nose.

The trio turned to leave. Star and Spud peered out of the rucksack and saw that the man was wearing a fluorescent yellow jacket with 'Royal Fireworks Team' emblazoned on the back.

The puppies wriggled inside the bag, ears aloft and tails thrashing. Spud looked at his sister, his tongue lolloping with excitement like it usually did at breakfast. 'Sis,' he woofed, 'I think we've stumbled on a royal adventure!'

'Now what do we do?' wagged Spud. 'We need a Spy-Dog plan, sis.' But before they could act, the bellboy had returned and picked up the rucksack and hurled it into a room. The pups heard a key being turned. *Not good*, thought Star.

Out of the bag came her head, followed by a wriggling body. Soon she had escaped, delighted to be able to stretch her limbs at last. Spud struggled. His head came out but his liking for sausage rolls meant he got stuck halfway.

'Quickly,' urged his sister. 'No time to waste.'

Spud wriggled like a fish on a hook and eventually freed himself from the rucksack. The puppies found themselves locked in a luggage room.

'One window.' Star pointed it out with her nose. 'Very high up. That's our only way out!'

The pups could hear a TV outside. The news reporter was thrilled to have been chosen to report on the royal wedding and her enthusiasm lit up the screen. She talked while pictures were beamed from a helicopter. 'A bird's-eye view! Just look at the crowds!' she babbled. 'Hundreds of thousands of people lining the streets of London to take in this historic occasion.' The TV cut to a camera at ground level, showing images of the royal couple, beaming and waving as they drove along the Mall. 'They couldn't be happier.' The camera panned in for a close-up of the bride. 'And just look at that necklace,' swooned the commentator. 'We're told it's been passed down through royal generations and is on loan from the Tower of London. Something borrowed indeed! And it's not only the bride. The Queen has also taken the opportunity to wear some pieces from the Crown jewels. A rare outing for such valuable pieces of jewellery.'

Star looked at her brother and gulped. '*Rare* outing?' she woofed. 'If we don't do something, it will be their *last* outing!'

'Plan A,' woofed back Spud. 'We split up. You go to the Tower of London. And I'll take care of the firework display at the palace.'

'What's Plan B?' barked Star.

Her brother shrugged. 'Plan A's all we've got, sis. So we'd better make it work!'

Spud already had a suitcase handle in his mouth, dragging it across the room. Then he grabbed another, which he heaved on top. Star cottoned on quickly and between them they started building a suitcase tower towards the window.

Spud wanted to rest but his sister wouldn't let him. 'We're Spy Pups, bro,' she scolded. 'We don't rest until the crime is solved and the baddies are under lock and key.' Luckily, her brother found some sandwiches in one of the bags and he attacked the tower-building activity with renewed enthusiasm.

Eventually the tower was finished. Star stood at the bottom and looked up at the rickety pile of suitcases and bags. 'Now or never,' she woofed, climbing the first few steps towards the window.

The tower wobbled but she kept scrabbling upwards. Spud crossed his paws, hoping his sister would make it. She fought her way to the top and looked down. 'Come on, Spud,' she woofed, as she disappeared out of the window. But as she jumped out her back leg kicked the top case and the tower wobbled dangerously.

No way, thought Spud as he ran for cover. The pile of cases fell with a huge crash and the door was immediately unlocked by the bellboy who looked in. Spud darted through his legs, waited a few seconds for the revolving door to swing, and was away.

Star jumped from the window and landed with a thud. She waited a few minutes for her brother but he didn't show. *I've not got time to wait around*, she thought. *It's getting dark. The crime will be happening very soon*.

She darted between buses, taxis and bicycles. *And horses! So many feet to dodge too!* Star sprinted along the riverbank towards the Tower of London, a small puppy in pursuit of a big crime.

Meanwhile, Spud left the hotel and turned left for Buckingham Palace. He wasn't as fit as his sister so he hitched a ride on the bumper of a taxi, waving at passersby. He saluted to a passing cyclist. 'Just off to save the Crown jewels. Duty calls and all that.' The cyclist looked bemused, her eyes locked on the hitch-hiking puppy, and when the taxi turned left towards the palace Spud watched as the cyclist thumped into a lamp post.

When Spud arrived at Buckingham Palace and hopped off the taxi the tiny puppy looked up at the vast house and gasped. Thousands of people were milling around. Spud poked his head through a gate and chatted to a few of the Queen's royal dogs. The corgis told him that the firework display was set up in the palace gardens but that he wasn't allowed in. 'We're on patrol,' they warned. 'Royal guard. And there are fifty of us. So don't even think about it, Sonny Jim.'

But I'm a Spy Pup, he thought. *A highly trained secret agent. I'm as good as fifty corgis!* Spud waited for the dogs to move on before he wriggled under the gate. *Nobody will notice a small black puppy*, he decided. *Especially not in the dark.* As Spud crept towards the garden he noticed an armoured van leaving the palace. *Yikes! The Crown jewels are leaving. I'd better get a move on!*

All was quiet at the Tower of London. *It's as the criminals had planned*, thought Star. *The world's attention is on the palace, leaving a gaping security hole at the Tower!*

The puppy positioned herself in a shrub at

the main entrance, nose poking out, whiskers twitching for danger. She shivered with excitement as the armoured van approached. The two glamorous ladies from the hotel were sauntering nearby as it pulled up. Two guards got out of the van and checked the coast was clear. One of the ladies approached a guard and asked for directions. As the man pointed out the way he received a karate chop to the neck and a knee to the groin. The other guard reached for his pistol, but baddie number two took care of that with a kick to his wrist, sending the gun somersaulting into the air. The weapon clattered to the pavement. The security guard was expertly felled and both guards were dragged away and tied up.

Very professional, thought Star. *If they weren't so evil, I'd be impressed.* One of the women opened her shoulder bag. Star crept as close as she dared. She watched as the woman wired up an explosive device to the back doors of the armoured vehicle. She kept checking her watch. *They've got to blow the doors at the same moment the fireworks go up*, thought Star. *No room for error.* She looked up at the Tower clock. *Five minutes to eight o'clock!* She wondered what her brother was up to at the palace. She crossed her paws for good luck. *I hope he's OK*, she thought. *And that he manages to stop the fireworks!*

Spud hadn't had much time to think. He had, however, discovered that corgis were *very* territorial. He'd fought off a pair with his best kung fu, but he knew that there were others looking out for him. He'd crept silently to the huge back lawn of the palace where a small team of people were putting the finishing touches to the explosives. It was dark but they were carrying torches and Spud watched as flat-nose unravelled some wire and connected it to a huge trigger. *Like I've seen on the telly*, he thought, *when they blow up a big building. He presses that plunger and,* BANG, *the fireworks will explode. And so will the back of the van at the Tower!* Spud could see Big Ben in the distance. *Five minutes to think of a plan!*

The seconds ticked by. Spud could only think of one course of action. He'd been taught that maximum distraction was *always* a good tactic. Spud spied a pair of corgis and barked across the garden. 'Oi,' he woofed, trying to sound tough, 'I've heard you corgis are a bunch of pampered pooches.'

The biggest corgi looked around, surprised. He thought of himself as a royal bodyguard. How dare a canine intruder call him names?

Spud came out of the shadows, stood on his hind legs and stuck his paws in his ears. He went cross-eyed. 'Cooee! Mr Fluffy Woofy!' Spud stuck out his tongue and waggled it at the corgis.

Within seconds the lead corgi had summoned help. Spud's blood chilled as he heard barking from all sides. *Scary*, he thought, *but exactly what I want. Now it's all about the timing*. A hooter signalled a warning and a digital clock started counting backwards from ten. The fireworks team ran for cover.

'Geronimoooo!' yelped Spud, charging towards the middle of the lawn where flat-nose was counting down to lift-off.

'Ten, nine, eight . . .' he heard the man chanting.

Spud's chest heaved. He could see white teeth coming at him from all angles. *This is gonna hurt!*

'Seven, six, five . . .' The man was looking at his watch, engrossed in the countdown. He had no idea that fifty dogs were descending on him from the darkest corners of the royal garden. 'Four . . . three . . .'

'. . . Two . . . one!' yelled the woman, pressing the button.

Star hid her face in her paws as a huge explosion blew off the van's back doors. The women and puppy cowered as hot metal fell from the sky. *But no fireworks!* thought Star, punching the air. *Go, bro! A million people will have heard the explosion! Help will be on its way!*

The women looked up at the twinkling stars in the quiet night sky. Flames were already licking at the van. 'W-where? W-what?' stammered one, pointing to the clear sky. But the other woman was already running away.

Star could hear police sirens getting closer but she decided to make sure that the criminals would be captured before the police arrived. She shinned up a nearby flagpole and tore off the Union Jack. The first woman was easy to deal with. She hadn't moved a muscle, and was rooted to the spot in a panic attack. So Star went for the runner, rugby-tackling her and tying her legs with the flag, before dragging the now wailing woman back to her accomplice. By the time the police arrived both criminals were securely tied and Star was standing guard over the jewels. 'Lock 'em in the Tower,' growled the puppy. 'And throw away the key!'

It took a few days for everything to calm down. Reporters from across the world wanted to meet Spud and Star. They were even invited to meet the prince and new princess. 'If it wasn't for you pups,' explained the princess, 'there'd be no more Crown jewels! The nation owes you a huge debt.'

Spud took a while to recover. 'It's the last time I pick a fight with fifty corgis,' he growled through a bruised mouth. His left front paw was in a sling and he had a very red eye. 'But it was worth it. You should have been there,' he woofed to Lara. The firework man got a real shock as fifty dogs attacked him from out of nowhere. *Wham! Bam. Pow!* Knocked the button right out of his hand. Fireworks grounded.'

'Leaving me to ground the other two,' wagged Star. 'With no fireworks, the explosion was heard across London, so I tidied up a few things before the police arrived. You should have seen the look on the policeman's face when he saw the Crown jewels in the back of the van!'

Spud and Star looked at each other and smiled. 'Priceless!'

CLASSIFIED

MISSION FILE

Ref: GM451/10/SCRTSNT

BACKGROUND

GM451 was almost run over by Stanley Strange, a computer genius who hates children but had a Father Christmas outfit in his car, which struck Spud and Star as odd. They were investigating his vehicle when he drove off, and they discovered that he planned to pretend to be Father Christmas at a large department store in London. He was going to cause chaos, and while everyone was panicking, steal the shop's money using his computer skills.

MISSION

GM451 was already in London with the Cooks, visiting Professor Cortex. Mrs Cook had taken Ollie to the very department store that was going to be robbed. GM451 set off across London to rescue her family.

SUMMARY

Thanks to the effective use of Secret Service equipment, Stanley Strange was eventually captured. GM451 received significant injuries. Again!

CONCLUSIONS

For the first time, the Cook children were never at serious risk – Ollie was with his mother the whole time, and handled the danger very well. Spud and Star performed excellently. But GM451 is getting too old for this kind of mission.

Poss. retirement?

Mission Log Extract

As Lara and the children hurried away Spud whispered to his sister. 'I've got an idea! Let's jump on his car with our muddy paws!'

Before Star could answer, Spud leapt on to the bonnet and marched backwards and forwards leaving dirty paw marks all over the paintwork and the windscreen.

'Serves him right!' giggled Star as she bounded up on to the roof to add her own prints – but then she stopped suddenly. 'Spud! Spud! Look inside the car!'

Star stared in amazement at a pile of clothes lying neatly on the back seat. 'Look! Red trousers and a red coat, a black belt and big black boots, a hat with a white fur trim – and yes, there it is – a white false beard. Do you know what that is?'

'Of course I do, silly!' said Spud. 'It's a Father Christmas outfit!'

The pups looked at each other in excitement, sensing the beginning of a mystery. 'The question is,' said Star, 'if he hates Christmas and children so much, what's a Father Christmas outfit doing in Stanley Strange's car?'

Spy Dog Secret Santa

Why did Father Christmas give his assistant less food?
Because overeating was bad for his elf.

What goes 'Oh, oh, oh!'?
Father Christmas walking backwards.

Why has Father Christmas got three gardens?
He likes to hoe, hoe, hoe.

Why does Father Christmas climb down the chimney?
Because it soots him.

Father Christmas was getting the sleigh ready, but he was worried about the weather.

'Looks like rain, dear,' he said.

What are elves afraid of at Christmas?
That Father Christmas will give them the sack.

What does Rudolph want for Christmas?
A Snowy SleighStation.

PERSONAL FILE

Ref: GM451/SPSCHL001

Classification: Ultra-secure core employee

Name: Professor Maximus Cortex

Appearance: ~~Old~~ Mature, ~~fat~~ well built, almost bald, wears glasses.

Personality: Extremely inventive, but often distracted by his ideas – to the point that he forgets simple things. Dedicated to his work. Fond of the Cook children, and especially fond of GM451.

History: Professor Cortex has dedicated his life to the Secret Service and achieved remarkable things with the Animal Agent Programme. For a while he scaled back his secret work in order to teach at the Cook children's school. Recently he returned to inventing for the Secret Service, trying to develop devices that can be sold to raise money for his research. Cutbacks, you know.

Professor Cortex heard his phone ringing and picked it up. 'Who's speaking?' he said.

'You are,' said the voice at the other end.

What did Professor Cortex get when he trained 20 rabbits to take a step backwards?
A receding hare-line.

Why did Professor Cortex put a knocker on his front door?
Because he wanted to win the No-bell Prize.

The prof actually has three pairs of glasses: one pair for reading, one for driving and the third for looking for the other two.

Professor Cortex was walking in the park when a man waved at him. The prof waited while the man came over to him and said, 'Oh, sorry – I thought you were someone else.'

'But I am someone else,' said the professor.

What does Professor Cortex do with dead chemical elements?
Barium.

CORTEX BRAINDUMP 0017

PROBLEM:
The perfect way to disable baddies completely without putting agents in danger.

SOLUTION:
A small pellet that bursts when thrown, and makes the target laugh uncontrollably.

NEW PROBLEM:
The pellets are quite easy to break accidentally.

NEW SOLUTION:
Great for parties that are a bit dull!

The big store was going to have its annual sale, and a long queue of people was waiting impatiently for the shop to open. A little man came along and tried to push his way to the front of the queue, but got shoved all the way to the back. He tried again to get to the front of the queue. This time he was shouted at and punched, before being shoved into the gutter.

He stood up, dusted himself off, and muttered, 'That does it – if they touch me once more, I won't open the flipping doors.'

Mum was out shopping when she saw a man pushing a supermarket trolley with a screaming baby sat in it. The man was murmuring, 'Calm down, Jamie. Keep quiet, Jamie. Come on, Jamie, don't yell. Don't scream, Jamie.'

'You're doing your best with him,' sympathized Mum. 'Is Jamie your son?'

'No,' replied the man. 'I'm Jamie.'

Dad was in the queue at the checkout with a big trolley full of shopping. A man came up behind him with just a loaf of bread in his basket. He looked at Dad's shopping, then at his watch, and looked hopefully at Dad.

'Is that all you're buying?' asked Dad.

'Yes,' replied the man hopefully.

'Well, you may as well go back and buy some more stuff,' grinned Dad. 'Because I'm going to be ages with this lot.'

Mission Log Extract

Spud headed for what he thought was a funny metal staircase. He'd never seen an escalator before. He started to run down it before he realized it was moving up.

I'll just have to run faster and . . . phew . . . faster! puffed Spud.

Eventually, he reached the bottom. Luckily, the next escalator was going downwards. Spud realized he could simply sit on the step and be taken to the lower floor without moving a muscle.

This is amazing! We should have one of these at home.

By the time he'd got to the ground floor Spud was quite enjoying himself. The shop was full of exciting sights and interesting smells. It was warm and bright and there was cheerful Christmassy music playing. Better still, on the ground floor there was a huge food department.

Mmmm, I can smell fresh bread and chocolate, thought Spud. His tummy began to rumble. *I wonder if . . .?*

'Who let that dog in here?' The store manager had seen him. He didn't look pleased.

Uh-oh. I don't think I'm welcome! Spud slipped out of the open shop doors into the cold air of the busy street.

Spy Dog Secret Santa

Mum come home from the shops. 'What do you think of this new perfume?' she asked Dad.

'It's very nice,' replied Dad. 'You smell lovely. What's it called?'

Mum thought for a moment. 'It's called "Tester".'

YouTube, Twitter and Facebook are going to open a website together.
It's called YouTwitFace.

Stanley Strange uses the word 'incorrect' as his password online. Then if he forgets it, and the website says 'Your password is incorrect' - he remembers!

Stanley was looking for a new computer and the salesman showed him one, saying 'This one's great, it'll do half the work for you.' So Stanley bought two of them.

Stanley stayed up late working on his plan, lying in bed with the computer on his lap. After a while he realized it would be much easier if he had a laptop.

Stanley spends so much time on a computer that he types **com** after every full stop.com

CORTEX BRAINDUMP 0018

PROBLEM:
The puppies can spy on people, but we can't see and hear what they do.

SOLUTION:
Cameras and microphones hidden in their collars - obviously.

NEW PROBLEM:
We've got way too much footage of the bottom of Spud's food bowl. And the puppies still sniff other dog's bottoms, which we don't need to see!

NEW SOLUTION:
Remote-control activation, so we can turn it off as well.

PERSONAL FILE

Ref: GM451/BDY0010

Classification: Villain

Name: Stanley Strange

Appearance: Tall and skinny, with pale blue eyes and straight blond hair.

Personality: Pretty unpleasant. Claims to hate children and Christmas.

History: A computer genius, Strange rented a house in the Cooks' village while he prepared his plan. The Cook children and Spy Dogs were carol singing when they first met him, and instantly thought he was up to no good.

Stanley played chess against his computer, and lost every time. But he managed to beat it at karate.

Stanley spent eleven hours staring at his computer screen one night.
The next night he made it more interesting by turning it on.

Stanley thinks all the time he spends in front of a computer might make his back problems worse. He's not certain, but it's a hunch.

What doesn't eat anything at Christmas?
The turkey, because it's usually already stuffed.

What's brown and hides in the kitchen at Christmas?
Mince spies.

Why is it cold at Christmas?
Because it's in Decembrrrrrr.

What's Mum's favourite Christmas carol?
'Silent Night.'

Mission Log Extract

'More turkey, Professor?' asked Dad. His purple paper hat was at a jaunty angle on the back of his head and he was brandishing a carving knife.

'I won't say no!' laughed the scientist, in a bright pink paper crown, passing his plate.

'What about you two pups?' smiled Dad. 'I bet you could manage another little sausage? Or a bacon roll? Or maybe both?'

Spud and Star couldn't stop their tails from wagging today. Thick snow had fallen overnight and when they woke up, the whole village looked like a Christmas card. They'd both found their stockings brimming with presents and now there was all this delicious food. This just had to be the best day ever!

Spy Dog Secret Santa

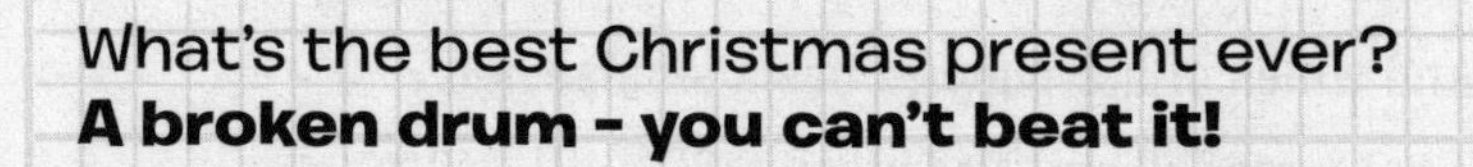

What's the best Christmas present ever?
A broken drum – you can't beat it!

What do angry rodents send each other at Christmas?
Cross-mouse cards.

What do you call an old snowman?
Water!

What's a hairdresser's favourite carol?
'Oh, comb, all ye faithful'.

'Ollie, how come you got loads more presents than I did?'
'Easy, Ben. I got up earlier than you.'

AGENT EXAM:
GM451 BACKGROUND KNOWLEDGE

You have ten minutes to answer these questions. No looking back through the files to find the answers. The exam begins NOW.

1) What do the code names LARA, SPUD and STAR stand for?
2) What is Professor Cortex's first name?
3) Name the Cook children in alphabetical order.
4) Who shot GM451 through the ear?
5) And which of her puppies has a similar hole?
6) What were Bill and Ned stealing?
7) Name the evil head teacher who took over Ben's secondary school.
8) What was the name of GM451's famous astronaut ancestor?
9) Who did Professor Cortex break out of prison?
10) What's the name of the rollerblading cat in GM451's neighbourhood watch?
11) What vehicle was used to chase the circus jewel thief?
12) Name the computer genius who planned to ruin Christmas.

ANSWERS ON PAGE 136

Final Briefing

I hope this book has been useful, keeping you awake on those long boring nights when you're sitting watching a hideout. Just you and the big plastic bottle (which you probably know how to use now). And you should have learnt enough about GM451 and her pups to play a full and active role in the Secret Service. I hope you passed all the tests. So welcome aboard, new agent! The only thing left is to decide what letter to use for your code name. You can have a P if you want.

ANSWERS

Page 14: Keyboard Konundrum
COME NOW THE BADDIES ARE IN THEIR BASE

Page 15: Brain XLR8R Test 01
1) A sponge 2) Because she's your mum 3) 5p 4) A river 5) ONE WORD 6) Your breath 7) Noise 8) Johnny

Page 26: Dog Tangle
Rottweiler; Dachsund; Labrador; Retriever; Beagle; Boxer; Bulldog; Dalmatian; Chihuahua; Greyhound

Page 27: Brain XLR8R Test 02
1) Five 2) The three oranges you took 3) 90 4) One hour 5) All of them 6) None – it was Noah who built the ark 7) Neither – the yolk of an egg is *yellow* 8) Can't you remember your own name?

Page 39: Museum Maze
See right.

Page 40: Odd Lara Out
D is the imposter – check the ear.

Page 52: Brain XLR8R Test 03
1) She's not dead!
2) Peahens 3) Eskimos live near the North Pole; penguins only live near the South Pole 4) They both weigh a ton 5) Halfway – after that you're walking *out* of the woods 6) Mount Everest. Just because it hadn't been discovered . . .

7) Today is January 1, and Amy's 8th birthday was yesterday – December 31. She will be 9 later this year, and *next* year she will be 10 8) A coffin

Page 53: Number Snake
If you've got your sums right, you should end up with 1.

Page 65: Step on no pets
It should say: Was it a car or a cat I saw?

Page 66: Brain XLR8R Test 04
1) Wrong 2) Second place 3) You could have: socks, stockings, shoes, sandals, stilettos, sneakers, slippers, skis, skates, snowshoes, stilts . . . 4) The match 5) Silence 6) The horse's name was Friday 7) Baby Bigger, because he's a little Bigger 8) He was playing Monopoly

Page 78 Treasure Test
The treasure is in square E4.

Page 79 Canine Crossword
See right

										B			
					C			S	P	U	D		
					A					R			
	A				S	M	U	G	G	L	E	R	
	G	H	O	S	T					I			
	G				L			W	I	N	K	L	E
P	I	R	A	T	E		S			G			
	E						T			T			
							A	R	M	O	U	R	
							R			N			

Page 91: Brain XLR8R Test 05
1) A chair, a bed and a toothbrush
2) He threw it up into the air
3) 'Ride each other's horse.'
4) No – page 76 is on the other side of page 75, so there's nowhere to hide anything 5) Pick up the middle full glass, empty the juice into the middle empty glass, and put the glass back where you got it from 6) A fresh ear of sweetcorn 7) An echo 8) Tree bark

Page 92: Spot the Shadow

Shadow E is the right one. (A has one arm too high, B has too short a tail, C has the legs wrong and D has no hole in the ear.)

Page 104: Brain XLR8R Test 06

1) Scissors 2) A chick in an egg 3) The letter E 4) 3 (Half of 2 is 1; 1 + 2 = 3) 5) Your dad 6) A barber 7) Nothing 8) It doesn't contain the commonest letter, E, anywhere

Page 132: Agent Exam

1) Licensed Assault and Rescue Animal, Super Performing Undercover Dog and Special Tactics and Rescue
2) Maximus 3) Ben, Ollie and Sophie 4) Mr Big 5) Spud 6) Valuable dogs 7) Dame Payne 8) Laika 9) Mr Big 10) Connie 11) An ice-cream van 12) Stanley Strange